THE WHITE REV

25

MW00355355

CELINE

SUMMER PROGRAMME

WOLFGANG TILLMANS
5 JUNE – 21 JULY 2019

MAUREEN PALEY, LONDON

REBECCA WARREN
1 JUNE – 8 SEPTEMBER 2019

MORENA DI LUNA, HOVE

MAUREEN PALEY.   21 HERALD STREET, LONDON E2 6JT   T: +44 (0)20 7729 4112
MORENA DI LUNA   3 ADELAIDE CRESCENT, HOVE BN3 2JD   MAUREENPALEY.COM

Curated by Charlie Fox　　**Sadie Coles**　　**HQ**

04 June–10 August 2019
Tuesday–Saturday 11–6

Sadie Coles HQ
62 Kingly Street London W1B 5QN

www.sadiecoles.com

BAD LUCK, HOT ROCKS

CONSCIENCE LETTERS
and
PHOTOGRAPHS
from the
PETRIFIED FOREST

Edited by
RYAN THOMPSON & PHIL ORR

THEICEPLANT.CC

HAUSER & WIRTH PUBLISHERS

2019 NEW RELEASES

Published by The White Review, June 2019
Edition of 1,800

Printed by Unicum, Tilburg
Typeset in Nouveau Blanche

ISBN No. 978-0-9957437-7-9

The White Review is a registered charity (number 1148690)

The White Review, 8–12 Creekside, London SE8 3DX
www.thewhitereview.org

EDITORIAL

As the UK remains in political disarray and large-scale protests against climate change gather pace, it's perhaps not surprising that many of the pieces in this issue of *The White Review* are bound by a sense of dystopia, whether real or imagined. We're excited to publish a surreal, disorientating piece of ecofiction by Korean writer Kang Young-sook, recounting an outbreak of foot-and-mouth disease in an uncanny suburban landscape. Estate agents leave bloody footprints on showroom floors; billboards sport images of the cows who are nowhere to be seen; and the protagonist – an artist – is plagued by desire for her mysterious double. This issue's roundtable, marking two years since the Grenfell fire, is on the subject of housing: our participants discuss overcrowding, gentrification, fire hazards and austerity, in a frank and impassioned conversation. Meanwhile, Christine Okoth's essay explores the uncomfortable reality behind feel-good capitalist narratives of sustainability, concluding that 'the goal of environmentalist actions cannot be the continuation of systems that rely on exploitation, dispossession and racial hierarchies... Fighting against the condition of waste and wasting requires a different call to action; not to renew but to revolt.'

Corporate irresponsibility also drives Edward Herring's short story *RLT* (pronounced 'reality'), a chilling – and very funny – piece of reportage from a future where therapy corporations brainwash bankers to laugh at tragedy. This debut work is joined by fiction in translation from Portuguese writer and artist Patrícia Portela, a dreamlike journey across unknown borders. Carlos Busqued's *Magnetised* is a gripping, collage-like true crime meditation, challenging conventional notions of ethics and evil, which gives voice to one of Argentina's most notorious serial killers: 'I don't see the devil as an evil being. I would say that the word "devil" has been demonised. I see the devil more as a powerful being who helps those who believe in him.' Taken together, these pieces offer grim insights into human suffering under the tightening structures of late capitalism.

Elsewhere, we're delighted to feature an interview with the inimitable critic Terry Castle, full of her characteristic insight and wit, alongside a conversation with Enrique Vila-Matas, in which he describes watching Marcel Duchamp lose at chess and writing his first novel in Marguerite Duras's apartment. And we are especially pleased to publish a series of poems by Charlotte Geater, winner of the second annual White Review Poet's Prize, following Lucy Mercer (whose portfolio was published in No. 22). Like our short story prize, the Poet's Prize is designed to offer a platform and support to early-career writers; the judges praised Geater's exhilarating portfolio for its assured and idiosyncratic voice, formal risk and sonic daring. This issue's cover is designed by Kaye Donachie, and accompanied by an extended series of her paintings and cyanotypes. In its subtle interrogation of the relationship between literature and art, Donachie's work embodies a perennial preoccupation of *The White Review*. We hope you'll find plenty in these pages that disturbs, provokes and entertains.

TERRY CASTLE INTERVIEW

Like many people, I discovered Terry Castle through her essay on Susan Sontag. Published in the *London Review of Books* in 2005, just a couple of months after Sontag's death, it was an account of the two women's 'on-again, off-again, semi-friendship'. In a series of hilarious scenes, Castle makes good on her claim that Sontag was a 'great comic character'. After skewering her subject, however, she comes full circle: Sontag, she admits at the end, had an enormous – unparalleled – influence on her, long before the two even met. In its messy, conflicted way, it's one of the finest tributes to anyone that I've read.

The essay is a fitting introduction to Castle's writing. Many of her trademarks are there: the lists and overflowing cultural references, where Dame Edna and Debussy sit side by side; the fondness for italicising and capitalising phrases. Most striking of all is her voice. Self-deprecating, warm but not necessarily nice, at times gleefully excessive, it's not the kind of thing one expects from an academic at Stanford (or, as Castle has described herself, 'Spoiled Avocado Professor of English at Silicon Valley University'). It owes as much to stand-up comedy or Dorothy Parker as it does to literary criticism.

Born in California in 1953, to British parents, Castle has been teaching at Stanford for three decades. Her academic work has focused on the eighteenth-century novel and lesbian literature, in books such as *The Apparitional Lesbian* (1993), *The Female Thermometer* (1995) and *The Literature of Lesbianism* (2003), a monumental anthology that she edited. In these works, and in her reviews for mainstream publications, she has produced shrewd, original criticism of great clarity. This can be unexpectedly controversial: when the *LRB* put one of her essays on the cover with the headline 'Was Jane Austen gay?', the fallout continued on the letters page for months.

Over the past two decades, Castle's work has taken a more personal turn. She has written a series of autobiographical essays incorporating a number of her fascinations – Agnes Martin, the saxophonist Art Pepper, the First World War. These were brought together in *The Professor* (2010), alongside the title essay which described Castle's affair with an older academic when she was a graduate student. Since then, she has written about gay marriage, outsider art and meeting Hillary Clinton; her current project is a critical edition of Patricia Highsmith's *The Price of Salt*.

This interview took place by email, over the course of a year. But when I was in San Francisco last September, I visited Castle at her home, a purple Victorian building that she described as 'the unintentional Prince Tribute House'. We sat and talked in her living room, the walls covered with artworks – including collages by Castle herself – and the shelves stacked to the ceiling with books, as her two dogs came and went.   DANIEL COHEN

THE WHITE REVIEW You've written that a strong personal style is 'the most difficult thing' for a female critic to achieve. How did you arrive at your own style?

TERRY CASTLE A dark business – no question. Some of the more mentionable reasons: I read all the time as a kid and by my teens and early twenties I had developed a precocious admiration for a small pantheon of kinky-magisterial female stylists – Austen, Woolf, Gertrude Stein, Djuna Barnes, Elizabeth Bowen, Iris Murdoch, Jane Bowles, Janet Flanner, Susan Sontag, Jill Johnston – all of whom (!) I obscurely imagined trying to emulate. Brigid Brophy made a great impression on me when I was a student – the all-in-one bund-ling of taste and wit and authority and hilarious bloody-mindedness. (Will she ever get the respect she is due?) However different in their mannerisms and preoccupations, each of these women seemed in some way fearless to me – critical, clear, rich in strange approaches. Flyting. Everything important conveyed with a sort of smuggler's flair. Depending on what was needed, they could either squash you or tickle you to death. I desperately wanted to be squashed and tickled – to collide any way I could with them.

It was hugely important to me, too, that none of my style icons (as far as I knew) showed much interest in femininity. Each had somehow managed to escape becoming coquettish, bovine, dithery or dull or otherwise bogged down in 'womanliness'. Stein and Flanner weren't even women. The usual male-female rigmarole left most of them cold. Heterosexuality might appeal as a plot device, but the reality was something else. (Unless, like Murdoch, you took brief copulatory spins on stiff-backed chairs with spooky Oxford goblins like Elias Canetti.) Most of my literary idols unsexed themselves early on, lived as lady-gangsters, or made only the most perfunctory feints in the prescribed direction. Lesbian or straight or else something in between, they all conveyed a kind of *not-a-woman-ness*. They were mannish and sceptical in a way I found gloriously seductive.

Early in my career, too, I think I felt emboldened to try to write in a similar way because I was so often mistaken – literally – for a man. (On the page, that is, though, I must confess, also at times on the street.) Not entirely my own doing, of course. My English parents gave me the ambiguously sexed, lager-lout first name I bear: it's not a nickname or short for anything. Dare one say

it brings to mind someone nasty, brutish and short? A football commentator, perhaps, with a greasy toupée and lots of back and nose hair? (*Castle* is perfect, however.) But therein, I guess, lay a certain charm. Experiments continue to show that readers of both sexes – even now – unconsciously discount or devalue what they read when they believe the author to be female. Who wouldn't prefer to be 'read' as a man under such stupid conditions?

Reviewers began mistaking my sex almost as soon as I began publishing scholarly books and essays in the early 1980s. I was startled and a bit put out at first, but realised soon enough that at least *Terry Castle, Esquire*, whoever he was, was getting read. (Bizarrely, this mysterious He-Terry was frequently accused of being a dyed-in-the-wool misogynist – a charge that made the morphological and ideological ironies of the situation all the more acute.) In the end, having cast off some of the cruder feminist positions I had touted during my goofy-to-grisly college years, I started covertly enjoying the mix-ups. Feminist literary theorists were always banging on in those days – often at tedious length– about how grotesque or pathetic it was when a woman writer tried to 'write like a man'. Accepting official approbation from men (think Marguerite Yourcenar admitted to the Académie Française) was seen as a downright insult to sisterhood – a banishable offence. Indeed, as rhapsodically affirmed by a trio of then-hallowed French feminist theorists – the frighteningly Parisian Hélène Cixous, Monique Wittig and Luce Irigaray – we would-be Amazon sex-warriors were not only to 'write through our bodies', we would somehow do so by mobilising our very own lady-parts – chatty little clitoris, lip-smacking labia, declamatory Mound of Venus, the whole kit and kaboodle. (Impossible on an iPad, of course, even with the Apple Pencil.) A lot got lost in translation, but I realised soon enough that the raptures of *écriture féminine* were unlikely to be mine.

I guess I never really saw 'writing like a man', however, as anything dire or shameful. I took the phrase 'writing like a man' to mean simply *writing well*: clearly, intelligently, forcefully. As far as I am concerned, everybody should write like a man. Man, woman, cat, dog. In my own case the payoff for being an oddly-monikered literary androgyne was considerable. Even now, whenever some clueless reviewer falls into the chromosomal-mystery-known-as-Terry-Castle booby-trap, I feel my confidence and conceit soar anew.

T W R   Your sense of humour is one of the most distinctive things about your essays, yet it's less evident in your earlier work. How did you come to feel more comfortable making jokes?

TC   When one is an untenured American junior professor, living on Ramen noodles and diet Fanta, it is safe to say that Revelry and Mirth seldom dance across one's threshold, love-garlands streaming behind them. So job security, when it came, was a psychological relief – as was the fact that after three years of unhappy academic exile at a fabled Ivy League university on the East Coast, I ended up living back in a gay and gorgeous panoramic city in California, my erstwhile home state. Teaching undergraduates no doubt helped, too: I couldn't just stand around stinking in my socket in front of thirty students. Cheap laughs were a way of connecting with nice young strangers who might otherwise find me freakish.

My parents were British, as noted, so 'English' humour and a spinsterish tendency toward sheer Vernon Lee dottiness and savagery also seemed to come naturally. One of my favourite film comedies of all time is *A Fish Called Wanda* – so English, so perfectly and farcically to the point. And speaking of Shakespeare, Basil Fawlty was a very kind mentor – a sort of adoptive father to me. I even had a brief but exciting affair with Sybil Fawlty. Still waters ran deep there. As I got older, gay male humour (as in camp) and Jewish humour both deeply informed the way I thought about things, too. Someone like Frank O'Hara could be a balm in low moments:

> *Well I was born to dance.*
> *It's a sacred duty, like being in love with an ape.*

I venerated the late but immortal Joan Rivers. Sontag seems to have agreed with me: recall the famous plaudit – 'a mind as fertile and majestic as Walter Benjamin's.'

T W R   One unusual feature of your writing is the way you capitalise certain phrases and descriptions. Where does that come from?

TC   Obnoxious Self-Importance? Whatever the Reason, I'm Not Proud of It. Nor its weak-sister-syndrome, my *italicising mania*. Both are jejeune writerly tics to which you are not supposed to yield if you want to be thought serious. Or, indeed, Thought Serious. But I can't help it. I live in a Well of Loneliness. Befuddled and in the murk.

I probably capitalise and italicise for the same reason – as a wayward attempt at comic relief. Typically, I aim to satirise or debunk some pretentious cliché or vacuity– often one of my own. But sometimes, admittedly, I get carried away by an urge simply to muck with the superstitious regimes of the punctuated universe. I especially like a kind of moron-counterpoint that results when you start inserting italicised lines of aberrant comic dialogue or spluttering cartoon noises – *whoa! eek! blam! pooh! pfaw!* – into otherwise supposedly austere intellectual pronouncements. Has to be done gingerly and sparingly, of course. As close to never as possible. Works best for me when I can set off the italicised 'rude noise' in parentheses or em-dashes: the thing then can function as a sort of rhetorical mini-package bomb. It's a flourish perfectly adapted, above all, for self-ridicule. You let some scurrilous alternative 'presence' push into the writing and splatter mud on whatever you've put on the table. It's like having one's own private heckler, a sort of cynical sidekick armed with dung. The dialogic silliness that results can sometimes be rhetorically useful, too: once you've emitted your puerile noise, the ideas you may *want* to get across, your real ideas, can seem by contrast sensible and sound.

T W R   Over the past two decades, you've been writing more autobiographically. What prompted that?

TC   Some overlaps here with the humour question. Getting further and further away from childhood was obviously a boon – prohibitions fall away and those achey, close-to-petrified muscles in one's neck gently begin to unlock. Disengaging in some degree from the academic world can also be good: having worked in universities for almost forty years, I've developed a sort of existential allergy to the pettiness and conformity endemic in scholarly life. I also dislike the self-righteous moral and political posturing found in much present-day academic inquiry in the humanities. Beginning in my forties I began wishing for a less alienating and passive-aggressive way of expressing myself. (According to my spouse Blakey I've now become just plain old *aggressive-aggressive*.) I also wanted to write more directly about subjects I cared about – my sexual orientation, for example. If one is gay or lesbian (or even just a sadly repressed lower-middle-class Brit) the desire to tell one's story can be especially pressing. It was in my case. I had alluded to bits of it in my earlier book, *The Apparitional*

Lesbian, but carried it much further in *The Professor*. Lesbianism was never a 'theoretical' concern for me. I was lucky to be living in a time and place in which coming of age on one's own terms – looking for some dream of ardor and intelligence conjoined – was possible.

Surely, too, the physical process of getting old can amplify the self-chronicling impulse. So many sad and ghoulish things start happening to your body in later life – and to the bodies of everyone you know. For me it all began with two thuggish yet good-for-nothing knees (I refer to them as the Kray Brothers), toenails hardening into stone, the permanently cracked and bleeding skin on my heels, pink rheumy eyes, feckless arthritic thumbs. You find yourself turning into your own bespoke Frankenstein's monster. Corpsifying. Worst is the fact that large bits of your brain go numb and fall off. Most days I try not to think about it: the sticky mozzarella-strands of plaque busy plugging up the blood vessels in my cerebellum. The universe seems more witless and unfathomable than ever and I less and less able to cope with it. If you've spent your life pondering the vicissitudes of existence – or even just ranking and re-ranking your top ten favourite pop songs of the 1980s – you may feel an exegetical urge to take stock: to suss out, if you can, what the whole misbegotten business has been about. Big themes you thought you'd settled a long time ago come back in surprisingly stark forms to haunt you. My mother died a year ago at 91 – an event, for example, I haven't yet begun to feel my way through emotionally. All I know at present is that she wanted to be the child, not the mother, and some might say the same of me.

TWR   How have the people in your life reacted to being turned into characters?
TC   I'm not sure 'turning them into characters' is exactly what I do. Yes, it's true that people about whom I've written have sometimes viewed my renderings of them as exaggerated or inaccurate. But I'm not making stuff up. I don't write fiction. However misguided the impulse, I'm always hoping to find some genuine psychological insight: the right words to capture those I write about as they *are*.

A rough process, admittedly. I find it hard to censor or sweeten abrasive events; friends and especially relatives have sometimes thought me disloyal in my attempts at honesty and precision. Speaking of my late but punctual mother, she was deeply upset, for example, by an essay I published in the *London Review of Books* about taking her on a trip to Santa Fe, New Mexico for her eightieth birthday. I had intended the account as a daughterly comic tribute – an eccentric but loving homage – but instead she thought I'd vilified her and railed at me, Clytemnestra-like[*], over several protracted telephonic tirades. Her rage baffled: I thought I'd managed to capture in some humorous light the complexity of our relationship, but also everything that I loved about her. As it happened – luckily or unluckily – there wouldn't be much time left for further shrieking. At the time of my perfidy she had already begun to lose some central swaths of short-term memory – an entropic development that dovetailed admirably, I have to say, with her life-long talent for instantly repressing events she found unpleasant. The next time I saw her in San Diego, a few weeks after she'd read the piece, she gave no sign of remembering it at all. Senility – her favourite Gentleman Caller – had been by and given her a quiet-down-Mavis pill.

TWR   What do you make of the recent boom in personal essays?
TC   I can't claim I'm averse. Banal to say so, but we are social animals, and most people are fantastically nosy about other people. I'm as nosy as the next and have always enjoyed rummaging around in the self-authored lives of other people – knowing all the while that autobiographers are appallingly prone to revise the past to their own advantage, deny complicity, vamp deceptively for pages, etc. Autobiographies are spinning and ducking games. But some of them can also be extraordinarily moving. The great ones have the startling bounty of life in them – even, paradoxically, when the writer has experienced neglect, deprivation, tragic losses. Sometimes the grimmest life-story can provide a weird solace. Over the years there have been a number of memoirs that I've found consoling in this way: Hazlitt's *Liber Amoris* (a lover's dark cult book, if ever there was one); Apsley Cherry-Garrard's harrowing Antarctic saga, *The Worst Journey in the World*; Vera Brittain's World War I threnody, *Testament of Youth*. Certain books have offered life-saving emotional information: J.R. Ackerley's *My Father and Myself* (likewise, his glorious *My Dog Tulip*); the

---

[*] Note instant bad-faith transformation of mother into literary character.

jazz saxophonist Art Pepper's *Straight Life*; Quentin Crisp's *The Naked Civil Servant*; Janet Frame's three-part autobiography, *An Angel at My Table*; Nadezhda Mandelstam's *Hope Against Hope*. Eileen Myles's autobiographical writing – especially the South Boston coming-of-age story, *Chelsea Girls* – has been a bracing and hilarious boon ever since I discovered it in the 1980s. A bizarre set of touchstones, I realise, now that I start to itemise them! But what each writer shares is a sort of uncanny openness and resilience, and a transformational tale told utterly without apologetics or squeamishness.

What I do think odd – to speak of the memoir 'boom' as part of a much larger and impersonal historical phenomenon – is how strikingly cultural attitudes toward the self have changed over recent centuries. We live in an era in which what used to be called vanity has become socially acceptable to a previously unimaginable degree. For thousands of years the gods and ancestors ruled human life; one judged oneself to be sinful and weak, even a lumpish ugly pillock, in comparison. Christianity glamorised the slavishness: Pride, readers of Dante will know, was the worst of the Seven Deadly Sins. The present-day tidal wave of memoirs suggests to me that we're beginning to see now the unintended fruits of a momentous inversion of values: the collective turn of the human species toward an ultimately unregulated radical individualism. Taking the long view, the inversion has come about relatively quickly – really, only over the past five or six hundred years. Once age-old social and religious hierarchies began to weaken and wither in the Renaissance and Reformation, it didn't take long for feelings of grandiosity and self-importance to steal their way into human hearts and minds.

At this point, the self-absorption has become both ubiquitous and potentially cataclysmic. As creatures now inhabiting (however unequally) the wealthy, wasteful, grievously overpopulated societies of the twenty-first century, we've fallen under the spell of an unprecedented and totalising materialism – the global flooding out of the spiritual by a seemingly inexhaustible shiny plenum of disposable consumer goods. One result of the commodity-glut has been to reinforce in us a death-dealing tendency to consider ourselves experts (*pace* Wittgenstein) on Everything That Is the Case. Not only do we begin to see our consumer choices – the infantile 'likes' and 'dislikes' of commodity-fetishism – as self-defining, we also

tend to regard them as prescriptive, something others should embrace, too. Everyone's a god now – a cosmos of one – or so the prevailing hallucination goes. Pop culture and the Internet have obviously made the self-intoxication worse. People compete to be recognised as 'influencers'. Humility is obsolete. And the banality or stupidity of it notwithstanding, everyone seems to imagine that *what they think matters*. (I confess I'm just as guilty as the next.) Such digitally-enhanced intellectual vanity – multiplied, say, by a factor of two or three billion – is going to end, I fear, in unimaginable conflict, suffering, and destruction.

TWR   Your essays are packed with your enthusiasms and interests – not just your scholarly specialisms, but music, Outsider Art, the First World War. What are your current obsessions?
TC   Each day begins with Peet's coffee and one or two hours of gloomy brooding on the unsavoury chemical *noumenon* of Donald Trump's hair. The Nimbus of Death, etc. Actually, no. In my dusty sixth decade, I have been completely overtaken by an obsession with contemporary visual art. I've started in fact to look like one of those awful little English children with the leering radioactive eyes in *The Village of the Damned*. Witness the piled-up copies of *Frieze, ArtForum, Elephant, Modern Painters*; the compulsive zombie-traipsing through galleries, museums, art fairs; the fancying of oneself as a budding collector – at least as far as one's non-plutocrat, multiples-only, little-girl-from-the-apartments income will allow, etc. etc.

Acquisitive fantasies of the moment involve works by a few far-from-random contemporary women artists: the stunning South African lesbian photographer Zanele Muholi; Chicago abstract painter Magalie Guérin; the elusive KOAK – extraordinary San Francisco virtuoso in paint and pastel; the rude and fearless and deeply gratifying Rose Wylie. Nicole Eisenman: *je suis toujours fidèle*, but you are out of my price range. Ditto countless pieces by the brilliant Mernet Larsen, Mary Heilmann, Ida Applebroog, Lois Dodd, Amy Sillman, Genieve Figgis, Susie Hamilton, Dasha Shishkin, and Angela Dufresne. (Not all of my favourites, I should mention, are female: I'm staring right now at a book of Sanya Kantarovsky's sublimely comic pictures of domestic infamy, psychological abuse, and people with long, freakishly curling legs.) As you note, I also collect lots of other things: vintage postcards, nineteenth-century tintypes, anonymous photos, Victorian cabinet cards, mug shots, art zines, worthless currency printed up during the French Revolution, lead soldiers, book illustrators of the twenties, utterly decadent yet beautifully engraved Ottoman Empire stock certificates, World War I ephemera, Ariel Poetry pamphlets, Shell Guides and 1930s Batsford books with Brian Cook's gorgeous cover art, Festival of Britain memorabilia, old or damaged signage, puppets, doll heads, nineteenth-century transferware, and lots and lots of so-called Outsider Art. Not surprisingly, one is eBayed and Instagrammed up the wazoo.

I've also begun making more art of my own. Did a bit when I was younger – partly my mother's influence – but now it's become a mad passion. Digital technology – and here my fatuous sermonising of a moment ago comes back to bite me – has made many traditional kinds of image-making super-speedy and fun, especially for bumpkins like myself. Drawing, collaging, altering photographs: one can now be as frighteningly prolific as one is shallow and derivative. Every day, a new *cadavre exquise*.

As far as writing goes, I've scaled back a bit. I'm currently finishing a project on Patricia Highsmith: a critical edition of her 1952 lesbian romance, *The Price of Salt* (retitled *Carol* in the UK). And at some point after that, I contemplate composing a long-unawaited little treatise on the subject of penis envy. (*I'm all for it.*) At the moment, however, I'm enjoying the wild amateur mishmash that is my (*ahem*) Artistic Practice.

TWR   Do you wish there was more room for enthusiasm in academic writing?
TC   I wish – enthusiastically – that there were no more room for 'academic writing'. Just good writing. Academic perversion needs to go. Ditto bogus American college-administrator terms like 'creative writing' and 'creative non-fiction'. That Proust, James and Woolf were 'creative writers' is something no one should have to hear.

TWR   You've written for a number of mainstream publications, but the *LRB* seems to be the closest thing you have to a literary home. How important has that relationship been to your writing?
TC   I can't quite fathom where I would be if the *LRB* hadn't come along. From the start I hero-worshipped the magazine's brilliant writers and editors (they were often the same people), the worldliness, intelligence and humour of the essays, the informal, stapled-together-at-the-breakfast-table look of the thing (soon to be graced with the late Peter Campbell's exquisite, off-the-cuff water-colour covers), not to mention the reliably madcap letters-to-the-editor page – so often reminiscent, in bizarre points advanced and fearsome rebuttals, of Jonathan Swift's *Bickerstaff Papers*. I've always enjoyed, too, the burbly, downmarket, squalid yet appealing Philip Larkin-'sex-pest' element to be found in the *LRB* personal ads at the back. Comparable *New York Review of Books* come-ons ('Harvard prof seeks superannuated sherry bottle for feeble libations') simply could not compete. See the little anthology they did of *LRB* personals a few years ago: *They Call Me Naughty Lola*.

TWR   It was in the *LRB* that you published what is probably your most famous essay, on Susan Sontag. How do you feel about it, a decade on? Is it odd to be so associated with that particular piece?
TC   Not odd, really. I'm grateful to have had the opportunity to know Sontag a little – from the mid-nineties to the early 2000s. And the stars had definitely aligned when I wrote that piece ('Desperately Seeking Susan'). The immediate impulse behind the essay, I recall, came from my sense that none of the published reminiscences and obituaries of Sontag I'd read up to then – she died in December 2004 and my article appeared in March 2005 – had really captured her well-known *monstre sacrée* aspect: the sheer larger-than-life magnetism and seduction, which she could apply, by turns, for good or ill. She could be a warm and thrilling and inspiring person (as I discovered); she could also be freakishly rude and unkind. Someone needed to articulate what everyone was thinking but not saying. It was also important to me to write something about Sontag's sexuality – at least as I saw it, from a certain distance away. Though closeted for so long, she had always been a major icon in North American lesbian culture – really, since the early 1970s – a fact that seemed both to gratify and dismay her. Most of the obit writers had simply buried the fact or given it only the most fleeting notice. I was in a position, again, to say something on the subject.

When the essay appeared, it is true, I had harsh comments from Sontag admirers who found it self-serving and indiscreet. I understood these criticisms and accepted them; how could I not?

The essay reflects some of the deep, deep sonar-pinging ambivalence I felt about her. I had begun as the worshipful groupie, but at the time I wrote the piece, I am sure I also wanted to poke her back a bit for the bizarre nastiness she had shown me – for reasons I never understood – on my last visit to her in New York. She had definitely provoked in me a mote or two of *ressentiment*.

That said, I have never regretted writing that essay. Sontag had an incomparable effect on me, intellectually, aesthetically and personally, and I wished to register that fact as best I could – if only in my own necessarily conflicted mode. The edginess isn't for everyone. In a professional sense, yes, the article made me better-known as a writer, especially in the United States. I found that recognition rewarding. But that was a fairly flukey side-effect, I reckon. My goal was to capture Sontag on paper as honestly as possible and make clear in the doing how inspiring she had been to me – and remains. I really didn't know her very long. Yet every time I've gone to Paris since her death, two or three times now, I have made a special trip to her grave in the Cimitière de Montparnasse (just a bit on from Philippe Noiret and his dog) to say hi, as it were, but also, thank you so much for everything.

TWR   What was it like to become interested in lesbian literature at a time when your university library hid Jeanette Howard Foster's pioneering 1955 book – *Sex Variant Women in Literature* - in a 'Triple X-rated' stack?
TC   Fun? Sneaky fun? Sneaky but educational fun? I've never been able to resist books and authors who have been declared off-limits for nice young ladies. Just gazing at the book's spine through the bars of the little 'caged stack' by the circulation desk – I worked late nights there by myself and the library at that time was usually a morgue – made it seem so alluring. And *Sex Variant Women in Literature* – what a thrilling title! A kind of Kinsey-era *Dykes to Watch Out For.*

Foster chose the 'sex variant' term, apparently, so she could avoid what was in 1955 – the year she self-published the book – the still-ubiquitous tabloidy phrase 'sex deviant'. Stylistically speaking, though, I'm not sure 'sex variant' is *that* much better. To my ear, both words evoke something simultaneously clinical and *a bit rum*. But who could complain? *A bit rum* can be good. For me in 1972, the thrill was discovering that Foster's book was in fact a witty, erudite, gorgeously written

work of bibliographic literary history. Discreetly 'sapphic' in sensibility yet never partisan in any hectoring way or the contemporary aggrieved sense. So capacious, too: she had read and absorbed over a thousand years of imaginative writing about love between women from a plethora of literary traditions. Granted, Foster unearthed a fair amount of sapphic schlock. Some of her artistic judgments are distinctly po-faced and tongue-in-cheek. But it still amazes me that such a humane work of scholarship existed at all and that I was lucky enough to find it in my brief 'butter lettuce' days in rainy Tacoma, Washington.

That said, I don't mean to be flip about my college library. True, if you sought some piece of Triple-X fare, you had to go through the super-scary rigmarole of asking someone at the counter to bring the taboo item *to you directly*. Not just the clerk, but anybody standing there, could see what you'd requested! Some dodgy 'Tantric erotica' book? That tome on urolagnia from the mouldy, multi-volume set of Havelock Ellis? Naff-zoological *Animal Mating Rituals*? Christine Jorgenson's pulp paperback transsexual tell-all? The diaries – god forbid – of Anaïs Nin?

But mixed in with the pawed-over prurient stuff were some rather more wholesome 'sex-cage' titles: various new acquisitions that by the end of the 1970s would be recognised as classics of the early pre-AIDS gay and lesbian liberation movement. I read them all. Gorged on psychologist Evelyn Hooker's pioneering essays from the 1950s; likewise, Dr George Weinberg's sunny *Society and the Healthy Homosexual*. (Both writers were instrumental in getting homosexuality 'depatholo-gised' by the American Psychological Association in 1973.) Jill Johnston's magnificent *Lesbian Nation* sat in the cage – like a lioness – alongside Maureen Duffy's *The Microcosm*, in the original edition. Ditto *Diana: a Strange Autobiography* (delicious and not strange to me at all). Dolores Klaich's *Woman Plus Woman*. My favourite among the inspirational 'period' titles was Sidney Abbott and Barbara Love's *Sappho Was a Right-on Woman*. Yes, a weird little brown paperback with the now-absurd late-sixties title (*sock it to me!*) - but also a bracing takedown of centuries of anti-lesbian stupidity and condemnation.

What it all suggested, too, was that Somebody Somewhere (the Library Purchasing Office?) was obviously *paying attention*: buying up this new and promising material as it came out and inserting it in a place where it might be useful. This unknown Magwitch, I concluded, had to have been Raymond, the antiquated, tiny-waisted, diva-ish little gay librarian who sat in the Bindery all day, reading the *Village Voice*. (Whenever I encountered him – me, pale-faced and droopy and usually pushing a book cart – he would glare in my direction with inexplicable loathing.) One had to give him credit, though. The unabashed pastel turtlenecks. The greasy yet tremendous blunt-cut fringe (or was it a wig?). He also had a six-foot-five-inch boyfriend, very handsome, like Peter Finch's beau in *Sunday, Bloody Sunday*. The age difference between them must have been at least seventy or eighty years, but the boyfriend was clearly devoted and discreetly picked up tottery Raymond every day after work at the loading dock behind the library. *Aye, Sir Raymond: those were the days.*

TWR   Your work has tried to bring lesbianism out of the margins, within literary studies and as a wider subject of intellectual inquiry. Do you think people now take it more seriously?

TC   Alas, I've become a bit of a same-sex wet blanket on such questions. It's true that over the past three or four decades literary scholars in many places have come to acknowledge homosexuality – male and/or female – not just as a worthy but a crucial topic of study. It's now fairly easy to find mainstream scholarly works that examine the gayness or bisexuality of key literary figures; literary genres historically receptive to the same-sex love theme; the rhetorical tropes and formal and semantic protocols through which such thematicisation has overtly or covertly taken place. Academia here follows the broad evolution of culture. Homosexuality is simply more visible now – far more 'present' and discursively available to educated men and women, intellectually and emotionally – than at any previous era in human history since the Greeks. Aspects of sexual life once considered criminal, morally taboo, or a sign of mental disease are now viewed by many straight people with dispassion and solidarity and often great sympathetic interest. Even with lesbianism – a phenomenon long conceptually opaque to many (as per the inane old question, 'but what on earth do lesbians *do*?') there's a new kind of *talkability* about the whole business. With the blonde and breezy Ellen DeGeneres in charge, lesbian talkability has in fact become part – dare one say? – of the global talk show.

Splendid news, of course. Yet I'm not convinced that it's scholarship on homosexuality that prompts such large-scale ideological transformation. Academic research, in my view, simply underscores cultural changes already in motion. I don't really believe in 'activist' scholarship. If literary academics are now inclined to 'take lesbianism more seriously' – as per your question – it's because of radical changes in the social and political fabric, not the result of anyone's academic research or scholarly theories. Has my own work changed anything? It sounds plonking to say so – an exercise in reverse-vanity – but I doubt it. For radical baby-dyke readers nowadays I'm far too past-oriented, too much of an antiquarian. Too literary. Meanwhile, a lot of even bookish heterosexuals remain uninformed and incurious. I reckon that the number of ordinary readers who bought that slab-like yet titillating tome, my 1300-page *Literature of Lesbianism: a Historical Anthology from Ariosto to Stonewall*, can be totted up on fingers and toes. Maybe not even the toes. Granted, Miss Philippa Larkin – amusingly tattooed librarian at the Willow Gables School for Girls – has always been supportive. But Cate Blanchett *still* hasn't called me.

A lot of terrific lesbian-themed writing, past and present, still goes unread. Of course, enlightened straight colleagues will now exclaim enthusiastically over one's 'queer' research projects, one's courses on 'Sapphic Modernists in 1920s Paris' and the like, but that's not to say they have read – or ever will read – the women one is always blabbering on about. Granted, a few sapphic luminaries – Stein, Colette, Willa Cather, Djuna Barnes – still elicit general interest. But as for true muff-diving oddballs like 'Michael Field', Charlotte Mew, Natalie Barney, Radclyffe Hall, Hope Mirrlees, Constance Fenimore Woolson, Kate O'Brien, Dorothy Baker, Jane Bowles, Sybille Bedford – even Flanner, Yourcenar, Vita Sackville-West, Sylvia Townsend Warner, Patricia Highsmith, or Violette Leduc – to name a wodge of them – you might as well forget it.

TWR   One interesting aspect of your work on the literature of lesbianism is the way it incorporates straight male authors: Shakespeare, Coleridge and Larkin, among others. With Larkin, in particular, you write sympathetically about the work he produced under the pseudonym 'Brunette Coleman'. What do you think these male writers bring to the literature?

TC   Humour, honesty, ribaldry, outrageousness – plus often a certain unexpected tenderness and fellow-feeling. Usually anything but the predicated venom. But Daniel – I must ask – do you really consider Shakespeare 'straight'? Or Coleridge or Larkin, for that matter? Coleridge's lady-on-lady seduction poem *Christabel* is sheer lesbian camp, I'd say – a real French-and-Saunders foray – and I think STC knew it. (One of the ladies, named Geraldine, is a sort of undulating serpent-woman with spellbinding boobs.) Larkin, as you note, had a fully-fledged sapphic alter ego – 'Brunette Coleman' – concocted (with help from Kingsley Amis) in the early 1940s. Brunette was supposedly the hirsute games-mad headmistress of an English girls' school – full of salacious warmth (unconscious) for her young female charges and a prolific author of Angela Brazil-style sentimental girls'-school fiction. (Larkin, weirdly, not only collected such fiction – *The Madcap of the School*, *Wanda's Worst Term* and such – but took a smutty delight in the genre's homoerotic undercurrents.) As I've described in 'The Lesbianism of Philip Larkin', he wrote a vast thousand-page corpus of works – fiction, poetry, autobiographical squibs – under Brunette's name. Though disdained by most Larkin scholars, the imaginative role-playing was formative for Larkin and inflected virtually every aspect of his later oeuvre.

I've been forced to conclude that certain male authors simply are lesbians. Thomas Hardy, Swinburne, Ronald Firbank, E.F. Benson, poor old D.H. Lawrence… Ernest Hemingway? – for sure. Much of Norman Mailer's writing, as everyone knows, is creepy gay male fantasy: I think he was trying to hide his lesbianism.

TWR   There's often something very personal about the way you relate to authors – when you say Sappho sounds like the kind of person you would like, for instance, or talk about wanting to kill Sylvia Plath. How does this fit into what you call the Boss Lady-Problem: 'How to cope with a larger-than-life female subject without gushing, grovelling or becoming abusive?'
TC   It doesn't fit at all! All it does is make it mortifyingly obvious that *a)* I contradict myself incessantly, and *b)* that I still have a fairly incendiary Boss Lady-Problem of my own. That I irrationally personalise books and authors. That compelling women writers – especially older ones – set off in me a crazy medley of emotions. That

Boss Ladies will always simultaneously terrify and enchant, require equal parts caressing and roughing up. That where The Lady stops and You begin is frighteningly unclear. (The title-essay in *The Professor* is all about this last blurring.) That life is oxymoronic. That, oh, yeah, the mother is everything. I'm now in my sixties, at least halfway back to childhood, and still at it: gushing and grovelling and becoming abusive at every opportunity.

A footnote on Plath: to grovel, as it were, in retrospect. The comment about whacking Plath appeared as the final sentence in an essay in the *NYRB* that had been drastically reshaped by my editors – cut by 50 per cent. A lot of mitigating context had been removed, making it sound far more brutal and reckless than my original. Okay, maybe it *was* a tiny bit homicidal. But it's true: apart from *The Bell Jar*, I really dislike Plath's writing. (I'm firm on *The Bell Jar*, though: had she lived longer, she might have found her real *métier* as a brilliant and scathing satirical novelist.) In the poems and journals she's always struck me as a kind of, yes, nymphomaniac ghoul. I can't stand all the heterosexual panting and simpering and man-chasing *à la* Rosamond Vincy in *Middlemarch*. Plath also strikes me as a version, known to mopey dykes everywhere, of an especially annoying straight-woman type: the one who flirts with you as a matter of course and then, when you're quivering with vulnerability and try to flirt back, indignantly denies having ever signalled any interest. Similarly, I find the sickly fan-girl death-cult around Plath – those bands of women who repeatedly vandalise her grave, scratch Ted Hughes's name off the shared tombstone, etc., rather off-putting. So *faff* on Sylvia all round. How's that for a sober, empathetic, persuasive, limpidly argued critical judgment?

TWR   What can we expect from your forthcoming edition of Patricia Highsmith's *The Price of Salt* – known in the UK as *Carol*?
TC   Oh, Pat Highsmith – how do I love thee? Talk about the Boss Lady incarnate. Not to mention the Lesbian Dorian Gray. Beyond ravishing in every photograph taken before her thirty-fifth birthday; afterwards, a hideous gargoyle rampant. (But always bomb-shelter sexy.) She could turn everyone around her to stone, just by looking. Tons of bad habits. By the time she died in 1995 she had basically pickled herself in drink. Smoked with depressive ferocity; probably also inhaled far too

much spinster-grade cat dander. Screwed gorgeous married ladies around the world. Caused endless homo-havoc. Pat has so much to offer! By the way, she wants to meet you.

The Price of Salt (1952) is a true cult book: widely known and cherished by lesbian readers (and also many gay men) as the first queer love story with a 'happy ending'. Most straight people have never heard of it, though, even fans of The Talented Mr Ripley (1955) and other classic Highsmith suspense novels. Yet Salt is weird and thrilling and sexy, with lots of exceedingly odd autobiographical backstory. At the time she began writing it, Highsmith, like Therese, the young heroine, was herself working in a Manhattan department store (Bloomingdale's) and had just had her own love-at-first-sight 'brief encounter' with a suavely enticing blonde woman who would become the model for Carol Aird, Therese's glamorous married lover. In real life, however, Highsmith never saw the woman again, nor did she ever learn her first name.

From one angle the ravishing love story that 'Mrs Aird' and Therese live out after meeting in the department store would seem to be an act of spectacular authorial wish-fulfilment. The 'happy ending' tag arises from the fact that Highsmith's super-hot heroines seem destined, after much turmoil, to stay together at the book's end. Unlike so many grisly lesbian characters elsewhere in modern literature – e.g., Jill Banfield in D.H. Lawrence's The Fox, killed by a falling tree, or Martha Dobie in Lillian Hellman's The Children's Hour (1937), who shoots herself after being accused of having sex with her fellow teacher at a girls' school – neither Therese nor Carol commits suicide, dies in a hideous accident, or runs off with a conveniently positioned male.

When one knows the compositional backstory, however, the book can begin to seem much darker and more ambiguous. As her biographers have revealed, Highsmith originally drafted Salt with an unhappy ending. In this first version (only an outline remains), Carol abruptly abandons Therese, precisely in order to return – not to her husband, from whom she is now divorced – but to a plainly villainous female ex-lover. It was apparently Highsmith's agent (herself a lesbian) who at close to the last minute convinced the novelist – amazingly – to trade in this gloomy denouement for something more upbeat. A major part of my task as editor has been to puzzle over Highsmith's investment in the affixed 'happy ending' – and take note of those points in the narrative (arguably many) at which her own closety, deeply self-loathing ambivalence about being a lesbian is still visible. Highsmith had a turbulent life and a damaged soul. The book is full of painful and contradictory psychic energy. Read superficially, The Price of Salt can seem almost floodingly rhapsodic, and one tends not to notice all the grim and very 'Highsmithian' psychological details (left over from the lost first version?) that remain in the book as published. But they are there.

Editing Salt has been arduous; one ends up with more questions than one can answer. Indeed, my spouse Blakey thinks that Highsmith – now a greasy sprite from hell in Levi's 501s – has been trying to boobytrap my work from beyond the grave. My goal is to get to the end of the job without demon-lover Pat – tumbler of Scotch in hand – engineering my demise through some unsavoury spectral means. I don't want my corpse rolled up in a carpet.

TWR   And what might we expect from your new project on penis envy?
TC   Penis envy? I said that? I must have been dreaming.

D. C.,
April 2019

RLT
EDWARD HERRING

FICTION

How Radical Laughter
Therapy Stormed the Corporate World
by Margaret Sweet

October 1, 2046

Since the age of twelve, Thomas Sprech has laughed at tragic events. It happened for the first time during a funeral, while he was enrolled at Kleinzschule Endelbraum, a prestigious Swiss boarding school located in the Canton of Basel-Stadt. The service was being held for a fellow student who had committed suicide a week earlier. 'When the details of his death were spoken, I *guffawed*,' Thomas told me recently, at the offices of his therapy business, RLT Ltd. 'It came so quick and so *strong – kablam*! Just like that.'

At the time, Thomas was unable to explain what he found so funny about the suicide. His teachers were less philosophical, and suspended him from classes for two weeks. Yet for the next year and a half – before he was eventually pulled from Endelbraum by his parents, and dispatched to live with his great-aunt in Zurich – Thomas's behaviour became stranger and stranger. 'He was always getting suspended,' Jürgen Miller-Strauss – a patent lawyer, and a contemporary of Thomas's at Endelbraum – told me in a recent video-call. 'One time he laughed at our teacher when she announced she had terminal bowel cancer.' Another time, according to Thomas's mathematics teacher

Inger Marten, he crashed into the girls' changing rooms, waving his genitals and laughing as they screamed and ran away.

When I asked Thomas about these events recently, he was unapologetic – even a little proud. 'I wanted to *see* people become upset,' he told me, his eyes dilated with intensity and delight. 'Then I wanted to laugh and laugh.' Now a slight man of fifty-six, Thomas is not yet grey – his hair and beard remain russet and thick – and his physical gestures are lively. He retains a strong Swiss-German accent, and though his English is excellent, his emphases are occasionally erratic. During our time together, he displayed an impish, sprightly energy and passionate sense of focus, like that of a very serious, very excited child. When he became particularly stimulated about an issue, he would stand up and throw out his arms to their full extension, reminiscent of Vitruvian man – a gesture that might appear threatening, were he not five foot four.

I interviewed Thomas on several occasions over the course of some months. Accompanying us always was his wife and business partner, Valerie Sprech. Valerie is eight years Thomas's junior. She is very slim, and very tall – almost six foot three – with a head of incredibly long, soft, silver hair.

When she sits down the tips of it touch the floor. Unlike Thomas, Valerie is elfin and cool, and remained totally silent during all the time we spent together. In fact, she has not made a public statement – or any statement – in the past sixteen years, having taken a vow of silence in 2030.

Thomas and Valerie Sprech are the founders of a controversial mental health practice called Radical Laughter Therapy, often abbreviated as 'RLT' (their followers pronounce it 'reality'). Traditionally, laughter therapies use humour as a means of releasing endorphins, and are paired with exercises such as yoga. But RLT is far darker, and far more esoteric: it is a therapy that teaches people to laugh at tragic, upsetting, unfunny things.

In their 2041 book, *Radical Laughter Therapy: a New Vision for the Future*, the Sprechs argue that human beings have been – and continue to be – dangerously conditioned by society: conditioned in how we think, in what we believe, but most of all, conditioned in how we feel. Most of us believe (or have been led to believe) that our emotional responses – our sadness, our joy, our tears, and laughter – are spontaneously occurring, and, what's more, inadvertent: that we cannot help but laugh or cry at humorous or sad things. Such responses, it's assumed, are programmed deep within our personal and social DNA. Yet according to the Sprechs, this is a lie. They claim that, over the centuries, Western society has attempted to limit and control how individuals feel, for the sake of 'engineering group assimilation'. Societal leaders, the Sprechs insist, quietly enforce this emotional consensus as a method of calming dissent. As a result, they believe, we have lost our ability for genuine, individual emotional freedom.

RLT teaches that human beings are innately free – 'radically free' – to choose how we want to feel and when. They claim that – if we want to – we can choose to shriek with terror at comforting childhood memories, weep solemnly at pratfalls on a sitcom, or laugh uproariously at sorrowful events. All our supposedly natural or spontaneous emotional reactions, the Sprechs suggest, are in fact false: when people cry at a funeral, they are not displaying 'real' emotion, but behaviour 'learned' after years of social repression and conditioning. We have all been taught to feel the same way as one another. But followers of RLT believe that individual human beings are capable of radically divergent emotional reactions. Hidden within each of us resides the capacity to 'feel for ourselves': RLT is about unlocking that freedom. 'We as a species have forgotten how to engage our emotional free will,' the Sprechs write in *Radical Laughter Therapy*. 'This has made us a sad, conformist animal.' But with RLT, they claim, 'we have a chance to access this long-lost part of ourselves, and, in doing so, become more assertive, more productive, and much happier people!'

*

In May of this year, Thomas and Valerie invited me to attend an introductory RLT group session at one of their centres. The session leader, Jonathan Case, has been a Radical Laughter Therapist for three years. When

we met, he greeted me with the words 'Hey there little lady' and a crushing handshake, accompanied by a giggle. Like numerous other RLT practitioners I have met, Case's conversation is punctuated by moments of forced, strangely inexpressive laughter.

The centre is located on the sixty-fifth floor of the Seel Building, the world's third largest skyscraper, in the heart of the City of London. It features conference-style rooms filled with plastic chairs and equipped with flatscreens, projectors and state-of-the-art sound systems. In each room are floor-to-ceiling windows that, when the blinds are whirred back, afford breathtaking views of the city's skyline.

Case, who is from Toronto, is a tall, well-groomed white man. When I met him he wore a white V-neck T-shirt and grey jeans. His hair is thick, dark, and curly, and his complexion is one of extreme good health – smooth and slightly tanned. He is thirty-six, but looks and sounds at least a decade younger. Case worked as an underwear model in his early twenties, before hearing about RLT through a stockbroker friend.

'I was a wreck before I met Thomas and Valerie,' he told me. 'Wasted most of the time. Like, cocaine, pills, booze.' (He giggled.) Case hit his nadir during a photo-shoot for Best Bachelor, a luxury underwear brand. 'I stormed out of the shoot, for no apparent reason, or so they tell me. I was drunk, my butt bursting out these skimpy boxer-briefs they'd put on me. When I'd sobered up a bit, I realised I'd been walking barefoot

up and down the Fulham Road for the last two hours, bawling my eyes out.'

Case's session began at six-thirty in the evening. 'A lot of the people who come here work in the area – they're lawyers or businesspeople,' he told me, 'so we try to cater to their office hours.' RLT is immensely popular among members of London's financial elite. According to a recent study put out by health think tank Mental Reach, 89 per cent of RLT clients work in high-paying sectors such as finance and law. Of the thirty-six people sitting in a semi-circle, all were dressed in smart business attire. (I declined to take part, and observed seated from the back of the room.) When they entered, Case greeted them, often snorting with laughter as he said hello, which visibly unnerved certain members of the group, many of whom had already looked sheepish as they arrived. A fifty-something man perspiring heavily into his cream linen suit asked if he could go to the toilet before the session began, and didn't return.

For everyone in the group, this was their first real exposure to RLT. Jean, a forty-two-year-old accountant from Luxembourg, was trying the therapy at his cousin's suggestion. Jean was six foot one, overweight, with a melancholic, hangdog air. '[My cousin] knows I've had problems in the past with relationships,' he told me. 'I get so down in the dumps when they don't work out.' When I asked him for an example, he sighed and looked away. 'I spent, like, twenty days in bed after my girlfriend left.' How long had they been dating?

'A month,' he said, and blushed. Jean thinks his romantic woes stem from his 'sensitive attitude.' 'I think being able to laugh at anything I want to – like being rejected – will help me toughen up,' he said.

Once the group had sat down, facing Case and the pull-down projector screen behind him, Case shut the door and paced in front of them. His assistant Emil sat at the side of the room. To begin the session, Case asked Emil to dim the lights almost all the way down. A sound system in the corner started to play brown noise, a low-frequency sound used to block out sonic distractions. The effect inside the darkened room was very calming – almost amniotic. Case asked everyone to close their eyes, and take the brace position: hands behind their heads, heads between their knees, staring at the carpeted floor. But before doing so, they would need to remove their shoes and place them under their chairs. Everyone did as he said.

Case began by gently repeating hypnotic phrases, in order to 'take everyone out of the room'. In RLT language, this is called an 'Individuation Exercise'. 'You are totally alone, in a deserted city,' murmured Case. 'You are the only person there.' Case began walking between members of the group, weaving between chairs. He brushed past the blinds, parting some as he went, and the pink evening sunlight briefly fluttered against the floor. The brown noise shushed like the sea. 'You can hear water dripping from every leaf of every tree,' Case whispered. 'You feel… content.'

This mood of languor and relaxation, to which everyone had surrendered (including, I must say, myself), lasted for roughly ten minutes, while Case softly intoned the 'Individuation' narrative. But soon, all this changed. With a gesture from Case, the gentle brown noise cut sharply to a low, distorted hum. Some members of the group sat up in their chairs, startled and confused; Case walked over and pushed their heads back down, hissing, 'Eyes to the floor'. Then he began to speak more assertively.

'You're all going to do something for me now,' he said. 'I'm going to utter something we call a "Trigger Phrase".' Case stalked the room, looking at everyone, making sure they were in position. He suddenly resembled a wild animal sniffing out its prey. 'Every time I say the words, "You, inside of you",' Case said, 'that is your cue to laugh out loud.'

The distortion in the music lowered and detuned, sounding grizzled and threatening. Case quickly barked: 'Thirty people have been burnt alive in a council estate fire in Gladcombe.' He paused. 'An earthquake in Tokyo has left seventy dead.' He paused again. 'You, inside of you.'

Most were quiet, but some laughed – a low, parched chuckle.

'In 1969,' Case went on, 'seventy children drowned when a bus crashed off a bridge outside of Kalamazoo, Michigan.' The distorted hum began to rattle and flare. 'In 2023, 108 dogs in the London area were infected with rabies and had to be put down.' He paused again. 'You, inside of you.'

This time, the whole group laughed on cue, louder and less awkwardly than before.

As the session gathered momentum, Case shouted out reports of murders and natural disasters. As he rounded off the details of mutilations committed during the 1937 Rape of Nanking, one woman bolted for the exit, hand over her mouth, about to be sick. Case did not acknowledge this participant as she sprinted past him. Instead, he simply walked across the room and slammed the door shut behind her.

The session continued like this for roughly half an hour, in one long crescendo. The music became louder and louder, rising in pitch, and by the end squealed through the speakers. (Emil covered his ears.) Case's prompts became more profane and sexually violent, his earlier pacific manner now transformed into a hectoring scream. Near the climax, he started addressing the group directly, leaning over individuals in their seats and yelling at them. 'Your father beats you with the steel wrench, you fucking *bitch*,' he shrieked in the ear of one woman, who visibly cowered beneath him. He turned to the man next to her: 'You piss on your childhood pet. What was its name? You can't fucking remember, can you? *Cunt!*' The man jumped in his seat. '*Can you?*'

The group's laughter had become more crazed and uncontrolled with every Trigger Phrase. By the close, they shrieked and cried like birds in an aviary. One participant thrashed in his seat. Another tore at her hair as she gripped the back of her head. On the other side of the room, I could see Jean rocking back and forth, moaning with laughter. A man sitting in front of me suddenly gagged and spat. I realised I had been gripping on to my pant leg so hard that I'd left a creased stain of a sweaty handprint there. And still, somehow, above the anarchy of human voices, I could hear Case screaming:

'Eat it, eat your own shit, mother*fuck*ers! Eat it! No one else will. *Fuck* you! Fuck *you*! . . . *You*, inside of *you*! . . . You, *inside* of you!'

*

In July last year, a research company called Omnidell conducted an independent survey for RLT Ltd, and found that the company maintained an extremely high level of patient satisfaction: nearly 86 per cent of RLT clients claimed that they experienced 'a high to very high' level of satisfaction in the therapy. A staggering 98 per cent of these intended to continue the programme indefinitely.

Theresa 'Teeny' Brompton, a former financial planner from Houston, Texas, went through a tragic ordeal in her early forties when her ten-year-old son, David, was killed in a road accident. Teeny's marriage to her husband (an English stockbroker) broke down, she left her job, and she cut herself off from many of her friends. 'There was no way of dealing with that grief,' she told me. 'It hung on you. I kept asking myself how *I* was allowed to live when David wasn't given a chance. All I could do was self-destruct.' (She laughed.) Teeny heard about RLT from her brother; she had already tried out several different therapists, yet had disliked them all. 'But from that first moment of stepping into the session room with Thomas and Val,' she said, 'I knew this was the real deal. The *real*est deal.'

Teeny now works as the marketing director of RLT Ltd, and helps produce video testimonials from patients whose lives have been transformed by RLT. 'We want to reach out with

experiences,' she told me. 'Stories, life stories, those can have a real result with people who are unsure about trying RLT out.' A striking feature of the testimonials is the social uniformity of the therapy's participants: almost all are white, live in London, and work in – or have worked in – high-paying professions. They all say the same thing: RLT helped their marriage, it improved their work habits, it rejuvenated their sex lives. It 'saved' them.

The demographics of RLT's clientele have changed little since its inception in the early 2030s. 'Even now, I guarantee there's no one on their [patient] list who's earning less than a hundred thow,' Charles North told me recently. North used to be a senior financial advisor for RLT Ltd until he cut ties with the operation in 2042, citing emotional abuse. North claims Thomas would scream at him every day – 'nearly every hour' – when he couldn't understand something North was trying to explain to him. Thomas denies these claims, calling North 'a fat idiot.'

A burly man with the faintest of estuary accents, North possesses the clipped, no-nonsense approach of someone who has spent a career reducing everything to questions of economy. (Ahead of each of our interviews, he asked to meet in a low-key café, or greasy spoon. 'I don't like frills,' he said.) He is highly critical of the Sprechs, believing that they 'cynically and greedily' sought to attract rich clients from the off. 'They built RLT to be a cult for people who could throw money at them,' he told me. But Thomas insists that the development of their client-base happened 'com*pletely* by accident.'

The Sprechs' first clients were Otto and Clarissa Parz, Austrian financiers based in London. Otto – who died from pancreatic cancer in 2035 – was Thomas's cousin. He felt sorry for Thomas, whom he saw as a misunderstood, if slightly eccentric school dropout in need of help, money, or both. He had not heard from his cousin for a few years, and jumped at the chance of seeing him again when Thomas reconnected, very suddenly, in the spring of 2031. 'We got an email saying that he was in London,' Clarissa Parz told me, as we sat in her spacious Notting Hill home. 'So sure enough, we invite him over for dinner.' But instead of the shambling down-and-out they had expected, they met 'this well-groomed, jolly person – with a *wife* no less,' Clarissa said. 'Thomas spent the whole evening talking about RLT this, RLT that... He's a very convincing talker. You couldn't keep him quiet!' Soon, Thomas was floating the idea to his cousins. 'He offered us one session, free of charge. We weren't so sure at first, but somehow, by the end of the meal, he'd got us to say yes.'

A week later Thomas and Valerie were guiding the Parzes through their first RLT session. A week after that, they had signed a cheque to the Sprechs for eight more. 'We couldn't explain it,' said Clarissa. 'We immediately wanted to do it again. It was like some crazy drug – but a drug that was actually *good* for you.' Soon, the Parzes were raving to all their friends about the therapy.

At first, Thomas and Valerie held intimate, one-on-one RLT sessions in their patients' opulent West London homes. 'The movement was still small then, and *very* exclusive,' Clarissa said. The couple had no therapy centre, and only forty or so clients, mostly bankers, lawyers and investors who had heard about the Sprechs through the Parzes' recommendation. Then, in 2036, the couple were introduced by one of their patients to John Crain. Crain is the founder of Stalk Enterprises, one of the five most profitable hedge funds in the world. A stocky, glowering multibillionaire, Crain started Stalk from his two-bed apartment in St Louis, Missouri, in 2004. He is intensely private, and is described by Charles North as a 'menacing' figure to deal with professionally. (He declined to be interviewed for this profile.) Thomas is so fond of Crain that he now refers to him as his 'godfather'.

In 2028, Crain was accused of sexually harassing a hotel cleaner; he settled out of court, but in the midst of the ensuing controversy decided to step down from Stalk and rusticate to his Somerset estate. By the mid '30s, however, he had wearied of life in retirement, and was looking for new projects to invest in on his own. He became the Sprechs' first major investor in 2037.

'[Crain] could clearly see something in [RLT],' North said. 'He's very much a gut guy. If he has a feeling for it, whatever "it" is, you can count on it turning profit.' Within months of meeting Thomas and Valerie, Crain had offered them a £25 million investment. 'That shocked a lot of people,' North told me. 'He'd done reckless things but nothing so out of the blue. People thought he'd been brainwashed.' But such concerns were quickly proven wrong. In 2034, the Sprechs could only manage fifty clients at any one time. By 2040, they had twenty trained RLT therapists, and over a thousand patients,

with five hundred more on their waiting list. Today, they run two therapy centres, both in the City. Last year, RLT Ltd was valued at £76 million.

*

Yet the Sprechs' origins are far from commercial. During the 2010s and early '20s, Thomas and Valerie were members of some of Europe's most radical left-wing political groups. In Switzerland, after flunking out of school for the fourth and final time, Thomas drifted into 'alternative living', squatting in abandoned apartment buildings and factories. In 2023, he helped found the Freiheitsbauerhof, a rural anarchist commune located just outside of Hamburg, devoted to traditional farming methods. 'Though many of us still admire more violent forms of activism, we wanted to create a protest that was also a kind of monastic retreat,' Hans Durling, an early member of the collective, told me recently over email. According to a number of sources I talked to, including Durling, Thomas was ejected from the group for aggressive behaviour towards other members, something he denies.

In England, Valerie – born Valerie Childers on Christmas Day 1998, in Harrogate, an affluent spa town in North Yorkshire – had been a member of The Left Hand, a student activist group at Leeds University, where she briefly studied drama. The Left Hand was known around campus for its provocative stunts, one of which – masterminded by Valerie – involved throwing a live pig into a lecture hall at the business faculty.

'Val was... special,' David Peach, a former Left Hand

member who now runs a bookshop in Keighley, West Yorkshire, told me. 'She was cleverer than everyone else, for one thing. She'd read more and could argue better.' But like Thomas, she was a firebrand and she couldn't get along with other people – 'and by "not get on", I mean, like, *pathologically*,' David said. 'She would sit there very quietly, look you coldly in the eye, then say something that would cut right to your heart. Game over – she always won.' In the end, Valerie left the group, citing ideological differences; her ideas for protests had by the end become 'too extreme for us,' Peach said. 'To be frank, I'm not sure how interested she was in grassroots political action.' When I asked him what he thought Valerie *was* interested in, he rubbed his chin and mused momentarily. He smiled. 'Burning everything down,' he said.

To Thomas, Valerie's defection was more easily explained. 'Like me, [Valerie] felt that political struggles could only take her so far,' he told me. 'It was the *mind* that needed a revolution.' By the late 2020s both Thomas and Valerie had shifted from anarchist organisations to 'radical-therapeutic' ones – mental health groups that sought extreme methods of treatment in isolated communities.

The future couple met at one such organisation in the summer of 2029, at a rural clinic outside Bloxham, a small coastal town in Norfolk. The clinic was called The Centre for Psycho-Panopticism, and was run by former clinical psychotherapist Marie de Vincent. An Anglo-French former clinician originally from Brittany, de Vincent had her UK doctor's licence revoked in 2022. Red-faced and wiry-haired, she can be seen in video lectures stomping back and forth across the stage, wearing her trademark black boiler suit. (When asked for an interview, she replied by email with a single line: 'Your publication and everything it stands for is COMPROMISE.')

De Vincent's theory of Psycho-Panopticism is based on the belief that human beings can develop a crude form of telepathy through group therapeutic exercises – including, coincidentally, laughing together en masse. In Bloxham, eighteen hours of each day was spent in complete isolation. 'You had to be in nature, away from everyone, with your eyes closed,' Catherine Upwell, a former member, and now a social worker in her native Glasgow, told me. But this was not Upwell's idea of peaceful solitude. 'Sometimes you were told the best way to meditate, or 'purify yourself', was to scream for hours. You'd hear people make the strangest noises from the woods, like animals.'

De Vincent believed in strict rules. Any slip, however slight, and you could find yourself booted out. '[Thomas] was really known in the early days as an enforcer. Almost like a policeman,' Upwell told me. 'It was his job to make sure everyone was abiding by the codes.' I asked whether this was a strange task for a man with a proven track record of social disobedience. 'I don't actually think he cared about rules all that much,' she said. 'I think he liked freaking people out. He could actually be quite frightening.' Upwell said that Thomas used to prowl the woods round the cabins at night with a torch, keeping guard in case a commune member was

involved in any illicit activities – smoking, drinking, drugs. If he caught anyone in contraband, he could become violent. 'There were people you'd see with their bags packed at the front gate,' Upwell said, 'weeping from a black eye.'

Upwell remembers Valerie as a quiet but forceful presence – an outwardly calmer, but no less assured version of her younger self. 'I found her *very* intriguing,' Upwell told me, leaning forward in her chair. 'Thomas was a common or garden bully, but Valerie had a special aura you couldn't really describe.' Valerie would sit on her own during communal meal times, and would refuse to engage anyone in conversation outside of group therapy exercises. 'She was so *within* herself,' said Upwell. 'She touched everything like it belonged to her. Even the ugly white water cups we used at mealtimes looked wonderful when she drank from them.'

There was one person, however, to whom Valerie had forged a secret attachment. Little did Upwell or anyone else know, but she had been conducting a clandestine affair with Thomas for months. 'I don't understand how it happened. I never saw them talk to each other, not even once,' Upwell said. When the relationship came to light, they were immediately thrown out, causing a bitter and acrimonious aftermath in the clinic. 'Marie didn't take prisoners,' Upwell told me. 'She took the relationship very personally for some reason. I remember after they left, no one was allowed to mention them. One man was refused food for a day after saying Valerie's name.'

For the new couple, however, the ejection proved liberating. Though it felt like a repeat of

their earlier exiles from school, university, politics and society, they were this time unmoved to join a new group or organisation. Instead, they had ideas of starting their own. 'Our feelings were not considered *permissible*,' Thomas told me, referring to the Bloxham clinic. 'And when your feelings are not permissible, you want to pursue them even more. That is a powerful feeling, one we use for RLT.'

Thomas and Valerie spent two years moving around different one-room apartments in London, with Thomas taking whatever job he could get. The plan was simple: Thomas would work, so that Valerie could research ideas for their own potential therapeutic practice. 'She went to the library every day, and read and read,' Thomas told me, 'searching for things that would get us *going*.' Thomas claims that though they worked out their ideas together, Valerie wrote the entirety of their RLT book in one thirty-six-hour sitting. (When Valerie took her vow of silence, she and Thomas learned sign language, which they only use with each other in private.)

One day, Valerie showed Thomas an article by an Australian psychiatrist called Stephanie Bishop. Bishop's piece, 'Accidental Laughter', concerned a psychological phenomenon called Unpremeditated Reflex Laughter, or URL. URL is an example of what psychiatrists call a 'non-personalised psychic event' – a freak spasm of the mind that reflects little to nothing of the patient's individual experiences or personality traits. URL events are moments when someone laughs for no apparent reason (often during awkward or embarrassing moments, like solemn events, or sex). Thomas was 'totally ener*gised*' by the article. But he had a very different take on what URL is, and how it functions. While Bishop believes that URLs are little more than examples of psychic runoff – slips, parapraxes, or unfortunate accidents of the unconscious mind – the Sprechs claim they are no less than the first step on the road to 'total emotional freedom'. When RLT practitioners laugh – Teeny at the death of her son, for instance – it is no reflex, but a chosen act, and the result of years of personal therapy and training. 'I realised, more than the Bishop woman, that this URL is not some knee-jerk of the psyche,' Thomas told me. 'No! It is our emotional free will *crying* out to us from the inside. It is our mind telling us: "Don't feel what other people are feeling. What do *you* want to feel?"'

A year later, the couple had developed enough of their research to begin approaching people they knew who might be willing to try it out. 'We asked our neighbour, who was a plumber,' Thomas told me. Did he want more? 'It was… experimental stages,' Thomas said. Having abandoned communal life, they were eager to pursue a broader clientele. 'We wanted *ordinary* people to do it,' Thomas said. 'Not radicals or anarchists. Those were people who had already seen something wrong with society. We wanted to reach the shop-owner, the accountant, the teacher, the engineer,' he said. (He laughed.) They thought of the Parzes '*because* they were the opposite of the people we had been around before. Our goal was not to court the billionaires,' he said, firmly, 'it has always been unive*rsality*.'

*

Recently, I met with Justine Newell, a psychologist and head of the Gloston Clinic, a charity founded to provide low-income earners with free mental health consultation. Newell dresses sharply in muted, autumnal colours, and bears a small, neat tattoo of a duck-rabbit (a visual puzzle that can be seen as either a duck facing sideways or a rabbit on its side) on her lower forearm. Newell is wary of condemning RLT outright: numerous people attest that it has worked for them and improved their lives, as the testimonials show. But she is concerned about its popularity among the financial sector. It is, indeed, a strange and, to some critics, unpalatable fact of the therapy. Lord Graham Meese, a Labour peer and chair of Mental Reach, has called it 'therapy for the 1 per cent.' This is compounded by the therapeutic practice itself, which is dogged by accusations of callousness, selfish egocentrism, and *schadenfreude*.

For members of a privileged financial elite – who for the most part remain comfortably inured from nearly all forms of depredation – to engage in acts of laughter directed at the tragedies suffered by others is, according to some, a fierce indictment of the movement's ethics. 'I seriously doubt the morality of the practice,' said Newell. 'It is targeted at people who are very wealthy. It gives them licence to desensitise themselves against other people's problems – or, as some believe, actively cultivate contempt. It is a project that teaches you that what you feel is more important than someone else's life. That, I believe, is the greatest charge against it,

more serious than any charge against its medical efficacy.'

The cry of elitism against the Sprechs is a common one, but when I brought it up with them, Thomas laughed and said he didn't know anything about it: 'I have never heard that *from* anyone. I think you must be making it up, *madame*, no?' I reminded him that he was asked the same question last year by Cathy Vinter, a journalist writing in the *New London Chronicle*, and that he became so angry he refused to answer any more questions. He laughed, again in that forced, pained way, so distinctive of RLT. 'Well, well,' he replied, visibly disturbed (he began fidgeting and rocking in his seat), 'I think that anger is a good *fee*ling, if you *can* feel it correctly; you just have to know how. If I ever get angry, it is never because someone has an*ger*ed me, you know? I am simply exercising emotive free will!'

*

In June last year I met Thomas and Valerie again, this time at a warehouse in Stewell, a town on the border of London. They had invited me out there to trial a new, 'very special' product they have been developing this past year, ready for release in early August. The warehouse was huge and empty, save for a single rosewood box, the size of an old phone booth, which stood in the middle of the bare concrete floor, surrounded by technical staff. Thomas greeted me effusively, leaping in the air a little and clutching me by the shoulder. Valerie was sitting cross-legged at the other side of the vast space, facing the wall – a distant black and silver speck. Thomas touched my forearm and whispered excitedly in my ear: 'Valerie is *collating.*'

The rosewood box was a 'Sprech Station', a soundproof 'therapy chamber' designed for something called 'self-service RLT': a way of performing a session of RLT without any need for a therapist. Self-service therapies – device-based, cheap, and flexible – have been popular since the early '20s, mostly as simple phone apps. But recently, the industry has started to expand with the development of AI-5 technology, which is able to produce more life-like programmes. These can range from free, easy-to-use phone apps like 'Master-It™', a distraction device for people who feel the urge to self-harm, all the way to more advanced programmes like 'Dr Nick', an avatar who offers one-on-one sessions simulating those of a real flesh-and-blood therapist, possessing the ability to recall information from past sessions and to make complex, analytical links between behaviours and symptoms. ('Dr Nick' appears on screen as a computer-generated simulation, wearing a dark green jumper and Perspex spectacles. He looks serious and concerned as he asks you questions about your wellbeing.)

The Sprech Station is at the most advanced end of the self-service therapy spectrum. On the inside, the chamber is simply and tastefully designed: padded on all sides, it contains only a small leather stool fixed to the floor, a touch-display screen menu, and a set of headphones. When you shut the door, it is totally dark and totally silent. The booth is built to provide a standard RLT session, the kind I'd witnessed a month earlier under the leadership of Jonathan Case. You sit

down in the brace position and don the headphones, and a voice recites Individuation Exercises and Trigger Phrases over distorted drones and piercing whistles. While Sprech Stations can be purchased for domestic use, they have been designed for workplace environments and public spaces. The Sprechs want a Sprech Station on every office floor, in every staff room, and in every available train station and airport. 'We want them to be as common and available as *toilets,*' Thomas said.

'This is going to change everything,' said Jonathan Case, when I caught up with him after the Beginner's Session (he was still sweating visibly). 'It's not only going to revolutionise our output and branch into every sector, it's going to *shove* it to all those people who say, "Oh, they're just letting rich people laugh at other people, like they're just elitists who wanna, you know, be allowed to laugh at babies dying or whatever." Well, those guys can shut the hell up now, they don't know what they're talking about.'

The Sprech Station marks a significant shift for the RLT movement, which until now has functioned more like an exclusive, high-end luxury treatment than a therapy for the masses. But Charles North doubts the Sprech Stations will catch on.

'If you tell someone from the City that you can teach them how to feel, when they want to feel it,' he said, 'you're going to get a lot of interest. A *lot.*' The therapy, according to North, attracts people who think it will help their productivity. 'People work like machines in [the] professional sectors,' he said. 'They're under great amounts of emotional strain, but they don't want

anything to get in the way of being productive. You give them a magic trick that helps them feel good about everything, helps them laugh something off, helps them be angry or assertive in the right moments, then they're going to pay out the nose for it.'

*

On 20 October 2044, a man named Clark Dowlinger stepped out on to the ledge of his thirty-eighth floor office, and jumped. He fell into the piazza below and died on impact.

Dowlinger had a history of substance abuse. The year before he committed suicide, however, he had gotten clean, and was by all accounts improving: he had taken up basketball, quit smoking, and started dating again. But a few months before he died, his friends and colleagues had noticed that he had begun to act strangely. Dowlinger had always been a bright and vivacious character – social, funny, sometimes a little wild. But he gradually became withdrawn and gloomy. A close friend noticed that Dowlinger had removed everything from his apartment that was red, and that he trembled with fear whenever he saw the colour. A colleague walked in on Dowlinger shivering and weeping by the electric heater in the corner of his office, complaining that he was 'freezing up in here'. People started to wonder what was causing it all. After he died, friends discovered that multiple payments for RLT sessions had been debited to his bank account. He had been practising for the past six months.

Dowlinger's is not the only RLT scare-story to have emerged over the past few years. In 2042, a loans manager at Welk Bank called Julia Sporetta was sectioned after she started threatening bank customers with a kitchen knife. She had become a recent devotee of RLT, having started the therapy a year before she suffered her breakdown.

With the advent of the Sprech Station, and the possibility that RLT will become a widespread phenomenon, should we worry about the effect it might have on the general public? Justine Newell noted the detrimental effects it has had on a number of others who have undertaken the treatment. 'When you start rearranging the furniture in people's heads,' she said, 'you seriously risk altering their personalities in ways that are potentially harmful. In the worst cases, you risk altering them in ways that are permanently harmful.' Newell treats a number of patients whose lives have been damaged and, in some cases, destroyed by their involvement in RLT. (Often, they have been forced to come to her because they've lost their jobs, and all their money.) 'Many of them started out very well,' she said. 'But after a year, they began to behave in ways that frightened everyone around them.' They'd burst into tears for no reason, or would suddenly find inoffensive things, like everyday objects – vases, pencils – terrifying. In short, they'd begin to lose all control of their natural emotional responses. 'It's not my place to reject a method that does seem to help *some* people,' she said. 'But, from my experience, I believe there are many aspects of the treatment that go too far.'

It is not difficult to detect trepidation when Newell talks about the Sprech Stations. 'Perhaps it's because I am hesitant about self-service therapy in general,' she said. 'But an important element of therapy is downtime from therapy – having the space to think and reflect by oneself. The Sprech Stations are intended to do the opposite: if you're an RLT patient, you won't be able to escape the urge to keep doing it again and again.' When I asked Newell whether we should be worried about the spread of RLT to the general public, she thought for a moment. 'Surely the scarier prospect is not that RLT is a dangerous scam, but that it really *does* work. And works in ways no one – not even its inventors – has yet comprehended.'

For Hattie Lamb, a former commodities trader who attended RLT sessions for nearly two years, RLT promises nothing but heartache and misery to all who engage in it. Lamb joined the RLT movement in her late twenties, when she was working in the City. But after two years of successful treatment, she began experiencing severe side effects. 'My problem,' she told me, 'was that I couldn't *stop* laughing. Once I'd opened the door, I found everything so funny.' After months of this ('feeling fucking batshit hysterical,' as she puts it), Lamb had a nervous breakdown, and was forced to quit her job. She has not worked since, and still suffers from debilitating laughing bouts. In November last year, Lamb sued RLT Ltd for £8,000,000 for 'life-changing damages.' A trial date has yet to be set.

Thomas is quick to reject criticisms of his and Valerie's creation. 'That Dowager [sic] man – that was an awful shame,' he said, sitting in their office. 'We sent flowers to his parents. We reimbursed them for all his RLT sessions.' He shook his head and tut-tutted to himself. 'Horrible.' But didn't reimbursing the family show some admission of fault on the Sprechs' part? Thomas sat up, askance. 'None whatsoever,' he said, surprised. 'That was all part of our *duty* as carers. He died because he was sick before RLT, not because of it.' (When I checked with Dowlinger's family, they confirmed that flowers had been sent, but insisted no money had been returned for the RLT sessions Dowlinger had attended.)

For Lamb, however, there is no recompense that could satisfy her. 'I was fucking *stable* before I went there,' she told me, tearfully. 'The only *issues* I've had are *because* of those charlatans. And now I can't go back, I can't be normal ever again.' She paused for a moment to wipe her face, then, looking at me straight in the eyes, said: 'Fuck. Them.'

*

In August, I met again with Jean, the lovelorn Luxembourgian from Case's session in May. We decided to go to a bar called The Tapster, situated in the West India Docks near Canary Wharf, and sat at a table overlooking the water. He was visibly changed. Gone was the portly, blushing, bashful man from before. He had lost weight, and arrived smiling and cheerful, dressed in a new pinstriped suit and designer sunglasses. When I'd met Jean before, he could barely maintain eye contact; this time, he greeted me with a kiss on both cheeks. 'How are you?' he said. Then, without asking for a response, he added: 'I'm amazing.'

'I can't really explain it,' he told me, referring to his transformation, as he looked distractedly out at early evening crowds of professionals drinking along the dock. Since that first experience of Sprech Technique, Jean has returned to the centre again and again, averaging five sessions a week. 'It's almost like I'm addicted!' he said, throwing his head back, laughing. 'I wake up and I think, "Wow, wow, wow." I'm full of this life-energy I've never had before.' Concerning relationships, Jean is optimistic. 'I've had some setbacks,' he said, smirking at a group of women at the next table. 'But the [RLT] training has really helped with that. Whenever I feel myself getting into a depressive mood, I feel like I have greater power to *tackle* it. It's like I can say, "No way, I'm not going there again", and move on.' He smiled, dropped his sunglasses, and winked at me.

Yet I found something strangely hollow about Jean's reversal in fortunes. Can people really change that quickly? If he had changed, was it for the better? With his swagger and laughter Jean seemed remarkably more confident, but somehow remarkably less interesting – less vulnerable, less thoughtful. It was as if his personality had not been improved, but chipped away at, or reduced.

*

Every single person that I have spoken to who is currently affiliated with RLT says precisely the same thing: that the Technique, and its creators, will only continue to prosper.

To their followers, the Sprechs have achieved something quite remarkable. They have managed to convert the tenets of anarchist politics, esoteric philosophy and medical psychology into an accessible (albeit strange) and, what's more, highly popular therapy practice. They have preached about the evils of society to the people who, ostensibly, were the stalwarts of that society, and they have convinced them (and possibly themselves) that a philosophy of societal transformation, and a method of helping people improve their standing in society (through improved work and relationships), are not incompatible. They have strung, tautened, and continue to walk across the tightrope between hollow commercialism and philosophical radicalism with startling ease. With Sprech Stations, the proverbial world – that of real pain, dejection, death, and suffering – will be their proverbial oyster.

Those outside the organisation, however, believe the practice will soon come to an end. Despite working for the Sprechs for several years, Charles North never participated in RLT. Though it has been a working rule throughout his career never to 'sip from the company Kool-Aid', to ensure he maintains his acumen and objectivity, he soon grew suspicious of the effects the practice seemed to have on people around him. 'There was always a man weeping in the toilet stalls, a woman laughing red in the face, bent over in the hallway. By the time I left, it was a kind of zoo,' he said. According to North, RLT's promise of radical human freedom is one big Trojan horse. RLT is, he claims, 'almost totally engineered for capitalists and careerists', and the Sprechs' endgame is, and always was, he claims, 'to make a fat load of money from people with deep pockets.' North believes the Sprech Stations will in fact 'kill the brand'. 'Their whole enterprise has been founded on hype and exclusivity, and has been pitched to white-collar workers. Now they're trying to branch out to the "common person"? It makes no sense. It's like McDonalds serving foie gras.'

On my way home from meeting Jean again, Newell's earlier response to my fears about RLT began to circle in my head. What if everything dangerous about RLT was not its freak side effects, but its intended results? The Sprechs' quest for freedom from the 'tyranny of mass-produced feelings' (to quote from their book), if taken to its logical conclusion, would result in a kind of interpersonal chaos, in which every aspect of our social lives – all those bits of body language, looks, expressions, and other unspoken emotional connections that make up the fabric of our collective life as human beings – would become unravelled. What if we became so inured to pain, death, and injury that we no longer felt a need to help or look after one another? What could people get away with if they felt no guilt, no sympathy, no remorse? What if, in David Peach's words, the Sprechs have unintentionally created something that could 'burn everything down'?

When I posed this question to the Sprechs, Thomas – unsurprisingly – burst out, almost as I finished my question, with a series of angry denials and counter-arguments. He insisted that people like Newell didn't know what they were talking about, and that surely only the creators of RLT knew what was good for RLT. And that I, by asking the question, had revealed how little I had really understood about RLT all along, despite the time and exclusive access they had given me. As Thomas fumed, I looked over to Valerie, who was staring out of the window. Throughout our interviews, over the months we had spent together, she had maintained her usual air of frozen neutrality, until now. Her face, usually so rigid, had started to crease, and her lips had begun to tremble.

Outside, it was a beautiful summer's evening in central London. A pink sunset, lowering on a skyline of large, dark-blue office towers, bathed the patrons of the lower-floor champagne bar below us, washed the bulbous dome of St Paul's across the street in its glow, and, farther down, glittered along the surface of the Thames. Later that day I would read that three rail workers had died on the tracks at Gorking Station, due to a misaligned signal further down the line; that a tobacco company, which sold clove-filtered cigarettes to underage children in Indonesia, had just opened their offices right across from where we had been sitting. As he spewed and yelled, and as small flecks of spit settled in his beard, and as the sun finally sank below the dome of St Paul's, and the river darkened to an inky blue, Thomas had not noticed: at some point, as he'd been raging, his wife had begun to cry.

LORNA MACINTYRE

Laura Macintyre's photographs of Celtic standing stones, Roman artefacts and domestic interiors play with the particular chemical magic of photography. By using light-sensitive salts to capture an image, and then dipping and staining the paper with soft drinks – Vimto, San Pellegrino and perry juice, or Darjeeling tea and black coffee – her silver gelatine prints softly subvert traditional methods. These liquids are absorbed by the paper, leaving the image with a subtle, sticky gleam.

While visiting Rome in 2016, Macintyre photographed the Colossus of Constantine, an enormous fourth-century statue of the emperor which once stood 12 metres high, now exhibited in fragments at the Capitoline Museum. For the series 'Solid Objects' (2016), Macintyre photographed Constantine's enormous hands. One, in white marble, points upwards to the sky, index finger raised in a prophetic warning. The other is a shell of bronze which once gilded the statue. Today it is ridden with holes, three of its fingers broken to stumps.

Macintyre's 'Much Marcle' series (2016) derives from a visit to the home of British ceramicist and sculptor Nicholas Pope in the village of Much Marcle, Herefordshire. The silver gelatine prints capture moments of material intimacy: a blackish tin of watercolours; ancient gourds on a shelf; the folds of a T-shirt. In her camera-less photograms, Macintyre's work is at its most abstract. Here, she exposed semi-transparent fabrics to light-sensitive paper, leaving diaphanous traces, like lucent blades of grass.

When Macintyre exhibits her work, photographs become sculptural objects, sometimes leaning against the gallery walls, or printed on silk and hung from branches. If the photographs are framed, the wood is stained with tea and coffee. She also constructs shelves made in materials that echo the surfaces photographed. In her recent show at Dundee Contemporary Arts ('Pieces of You Are Here', 2018), her photographs of Scottish standing stones were exhibited on shelves made of black stone. The series included an image of the Serpent Stone, which stands in the village of Aberlemno, Angus, and is covered in symbols of unknown meaning: a mirror and a comb, a double disc, a snake on a rod – the traces of a lost civilisation.

PLATES

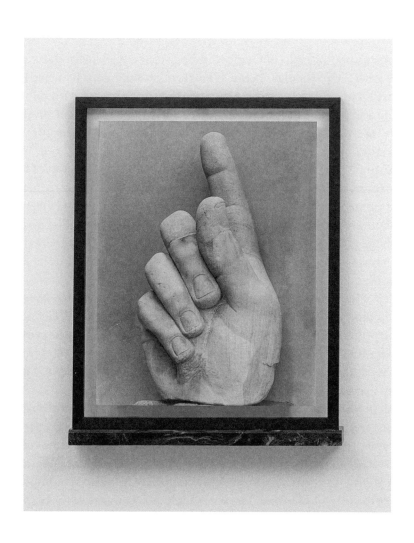

LEO BOIX

CHARM FOR A JOURNEY (A MISTRANSLATION)
'Ic me on pisse gyrde beluce and on godes helde bebeode'

With this toad I inscribe a circle,
and trust to the grace of Odd,
against the sore wound, the raw night,
the stinking fear,
against the swarm of horror none can spare,
even even slinking into the gland.

I sing a victory charm, lift a victory scorch,
worst-victory, victory of seeds,
let them help now.
Let no ocean hinder me, or heated enemy
beat me slow.

Let faith not hover hover above my life,
but keep me safe safe.

A RED HORSE

The pills have arrived.
They came all the way
from Boston to Buenos Aires.

He is waiting in his stained armchair.
Head down, rheumy,
constantly looking at his watch.
Ya no puede ver.

He fell twice, last time
in the middle of the kitchen,
bruising his jaw.

There is a lump on his neck
in the shape of a trilobite.
It grows at night,
when he's dreaming.

He thinks drugs
have been concocted for him
by old witches.
Ha dejado de hablar.

He waits, facing the door ajar,
giving his back to giant birds
that steal his unripe blue grapes.

A stone path leads
to his tool shed
at the back of the courtyard,
now abandoned.

The radio is constant.
Midday overcooks bedding plants.
He dreams of a garden he visited long ago,
and a red horse trotting in circles.

BALLAD OF A HAPPY IMMIGRANT
after Louis MacNeice

In the beginning there was a garden and a boy
who counted ants, dug for bulbs, all these he enjoyed.

Come back a man or never come

Father greased the Peugeot, his blasting radio
of 80s techno on. Learn. One day you'll need to know.

Come back a man or never come

The Spaniel dog under the kitchen table,
the endless heat, the dusty sparrows on hanging cables.

Come back a man or never come

Mother's dresses of palm leaves, her sandals.
The day she left they took her things. I lit a candle.

Come back a man or never come

Father dressed younger, and then remarried
after a loved sweet wife he quickly buried.

Come back a man or never come

We moved two times, from south to north
some things we took, some we forgot.

Come back a man or never come

The sisters shared a fuchsia room, few loves
I found a corner where I hid my joys.

Come back a man or never come

I went on trains to school and back
at home the fights, burnt stakes, news cracks.

Come back a man or never come

The night I left I gave some clues
look out for me, my ties, my shoes.

Come back a man or never come

The shared old flat in Knaresborough Court,
six a room, a kitchenette, my home of sorts.

Come back a man or never come

My lousy English. Searched out for words,
at least I still could communicate with birds.

Come back a man or never come

I met few men, went out to clubs, some were smarter
than others. And one night at the NFT, I met the artist.

Come back a man or never come

The daily trips to Hampstead Heath, late coffees in Soho
we kissed in Russell Square, a builder shouted: *You two, homos!*

Come back a man or never come

We moved together by the flower market.
Our tiny flat on Columbia Road. A new life had started.

Come back a man or never come

Long distance phone-calls. Dad and his orchids,
his health, his lungs. The chats more morbid.

Come back a man or never come

I nursed him a week. His bloody coughs.
And as he died my London flight took off.

Come back a man or never come

In seaside Deal we found some peace,
you drew till late, I wrote cinquaines, planted dwarf trees.

Come back a man or never come

Now I swim and swim, come sun or hail
the sea my friend, my foe, this holy Grail.

Come back a man or never come

And if they ask: Is this your place?
I say... Well, yes, my final base.

Come back a man or never come

CLOVER

I told him before leaving: keep a four-leafed clover at home. Wear it like a
posy. It will bring good fortune. He asked me to stay the night with him, take
care his tubes, needles were all connected to his drying skin. I put the local
radio on, lowered the volume for him to fall asleep. I caressed his ashen hair.
He made a sudden sign with his hand, as if I could now go. Then, as I was
standing up next to his emergency bed, I heard him saying in a low voice:
But first leave your thin shadow by the door.

THE PROMISE OF RENEWAL
CHRISTINE OKOTH

If you passed London's Old Street in the summer of 2018, you will have seen a usually bare piece of land near the roundabout adorned with a giant sculpture of a wave, constructed entirely out of plastic waste. The installation was composed of familiar detritus: empty milk containers, grocery bags and outdoor furniture. But unlike those plastics floating in the world's oceans or entering household recycling bins every day, the bags and bottles that made up the plastic wave had been carefully selected and assembled to replicate the shape and hues of an oceanic phenomenon. The Wave of Waste was the work of the beer company Corona. Surrounding the sculpture were three large billboards. One depicted a surfer; the others advertised the Mexican beer brand and their commitment to keeping the picturesque beaches frequented by their ideal consumers free from plastic. On closer inspection, the surfer was revealed to be the Australian actor Chris Hemsworth, a plastic wave looming over him.

The actor, formerly of *Home and Away* fame and now best known for his role in Marvel's *Avengers* franchise, is one of six ambassadors for Corona's partnership with the environmental non-profit Parley for the Oceans. In promotional photographs and videos, celebrities appear alongside local volunteers, picking up plastic waste from one of the 100 island beaches selected as the symbolic examples of Parley and Corona's environmentalist efforts. The installation at Old Street roundabout was itself constructed out of waste collected from a beach in Sussex; Londoners also had the option to participate in the broader Parley strategy by dropping off their own plastic waste, in order to become part of the sculpture. In Parley's vision, everyone has a small yet important part to play in the fight against plastics pollution. Movie stars, commuters and island residents become equal participants in a quest to rebuild untouched natural idylls around the world, as though the act of picking up a single plastic bag can reverse decades of wilful destruction.

Narratives like these, which tell stories of individual action, shared responsibility and small-scale intervention, permeate contemporary environmentalist practice. From reusable coffee cups to cycle-to-work schemes, the narratives surrounding contemporary sustainability reduce the seemingly impossible task of halting and reversing environmental degradation to a series of small, incremental changes. Some emphasise the role that consumers can play in advancing environmentalist causes. Others place corporations at their centre, promoting the business opportunities offered by innovation and eco-friendly production. Sometimes, multiple narratives of sustainability come together in a pastiche of misdirected micro-interventions. Parley for the Oceans is one such example.

The charity promotes a three-pillar approach to ridding the world's oceans of plastic waste: Avoid, Intercept, Redesign (AIR). Clean-up operations, which intercept plastic waste by collecting it on the beach before it can be dragged into the ocean, represent only the second of these tenets. The first – Avoid – also translates into a fairly straightforward refusal to interact with single-use plastics on a day-to-day basis. Redesign, however, refers to an ambitious effort on the charity's part to develop alternatives to single-use plastics. Parley's answer is their patented, upcycled Ocean Plastic™, a product that can be used to make reusable bottles, sunglasses and textiles. For the partnership with Corona, Ocean Plastic™ was used to produce a Hawaiian shirt. An ongoing collaboration between Parley and sportswear brand Adidas includes a pair of luxury sneakers made from an estimated eleven plastic bottles. By purchasing products made from upcycled waste, it's implied, brand loyalists can consume their way to sustainability.

A photograph depicting Ocean Plastic's™ evolutionary stages appears in various forms across Parley's website. Though its different iterations compress or extend the upcycling process, the overarching narrative of the image remains consistent. It tells a story of waste turned into resource, of garbage turned prized possession. Against a minimalist white background, the transformation of waste into sustainable consumer products begins with a bottle amongst a bed of broken plastic. To its right lies a handful of blue plastic shards. Those shards become small pellets, which are then turned into a roll of thread. At the end of the frame sits a bottle encased in a fabric holder of yet another shade of blue. Like the roundabout's plastic wave, sustainability here comes in comforting, clean hues. No shard is spilling over, no pellet out of place. Like the closed loop of the recycling symbol – those green arrows in a triangular shape that point only to other arrows – Ocean Plastic™ promises the complete elimination of waste through its reintegration into cycles of production and consumption. Ocean Plastic's™ single-image origin myth insists that sustainability can be tidy and beautiful; a matter of imagining new ways of consuming and producing, rather than addressing the practice of consumption itself.

This visual representation of recycling contains a latent political conservatism. Parley's condensed representation of upcycling confines affective responses to environmental destruction – such as shock, anger, and fear – within a single photographic frame. What falls out of the frame, namely the actual modes of production that turn plastic bottles into upcycled textiles, also falls outside of the narrative of sustainability being propagated here. In its simplicity, the image perpetuates yet another pervasive narrative of renewal, one of a recycling technology so sophisticated that it need not be represented. Recycling, the image seems to say, is not an industry but a creative project. In this particular account of sustainability, environmental crisis requires acts of radical imagination that are of a technological, not political, nature. Within that same narrative, plastics pollution in the world's oceans becomes a challenge rather than an indictment, to be confronted and ultimately triumphed over. Even the aesthetic qualities of Ocean Plastic's™ evolutionary stages suggest that Parley's start-up mentality is motivated more by continuity than disruption. Through the choice of that uniformly blue colour palette, plastic is made to look like the oceans it is actively contaminating. In its recycled form, plastic and its conditions of production become a natural part of the world, accepted as necessary but no longer evil.

*

From corporate partnerships to celebrity documentaries, the problem of plastics pollution has, in recent decades, become an environmentalist *cause célèbre*. Whether due to the popularity of environmental documentaries, the global panic around microbeads or the discovery of the Great Pacific Garbage Patch in the late 1980s, at some point in the last fifty years the dangers of single-use plastics infiltrated the public consciousness, directing both media attention and corporate funding towards efforts to solve the plastics crisis. As is the case with Parley for the Oceans, the idea of recycling often features either as the solution to plastic waste or as a central component of a larger zero-waste strategy. The Ocean Cleanup Project, an environmental start-up founded in 2013, has raised over $20 million to construct a device that would collect the plastic waste on the ocean's surface. Its boy-genius founder Boyan Slat, who was recently profiled in the *New Yorker*, claims that any plastics collected in its oceanic missions will be 'processed on land and recycled'. Details are, once again, scant. Where or how these collected materials are recycled is unclear, especially as the device (Wilson) has collected little actual plastic on its missions to date.

This is not to say that no media efforts have been made to represent the recycling process itself. In the UK, the treatment of recycling in the BBC's three-part documentary series *Hugh's War on Waste* is perhaps most telling for the way it avoids the subject of human labour. The series follows celebrity chef turned zero-waste crusader Hugh Fearnley-Whittingstall as he investigates the societal ill of food dumping. Airing throughout 2015 and 2016, *Hugh's War on Waste* follows its host as he embarks on a midnight dumpster-diving mission, slides down a mountain of discarded clothes at a shopping centre, and teaches the bemused residents of Prestwich in Greater Manchester how to reduce their food waste. The show's tone is one of deliberate condescension, which is nowhere more pronounced than in a sequence that takes place at a local Materials Recovery Facility (MRF). Hugh is sure that a tour of a plant in which recyclables are sorted and packaged for transportation should convince even the most sceptical of Prestwich residents that there are real benefits to becoming a good recycler.

Arriving at the plant, we watch as Hugh points out the various technological feats the MRF achieves. Look, he tells his tour participants, this machine uses lasers to determine which plastics belong together. Sometimes he gestures towards one or two men, at the far-left of the screen, who sort waste in the background as Hugh proselytises about the magic of turning plastic waste into plastic products. The positioning of the workers at the peripheries of the frame, and Hugh's lack of interest in their labour, signal to the viewer that the plant's employees should not be considered essential components of the MRF. Instead, host and camera repeatedly direct attention to the machine itself. Who, the documentary suggests, could be interested in the work of human hands in the presence of laser technology?

As the tour group leaves the MRF, every Prestwich resident expresses doubts about the facility's effectiveness. They ask some important questions. What happens to the plastic once it has been sorted and packaged into large bales? Aren't these still the same materials that were discarded in the first place? How are these bottles transformed into new objects? Hugh appears momentarily perturbed. Then, he leads them to a container, located in another part of the site. This variation on the 'pop-up' mall is stocked with items made from recycled waste. There are children's toys, a rain jacket, a fixed-gear bicycle. An intern is probably responsible for the makeshift paper print-outs listing the number of recyclable materials used in the production of each item. This display of sustainable consumption is what it takes for Hugh's participants to turn a corner. Their doubts dispelled once and for all, the sceptics of Prestwich become recycling advocates. They promise to do better.

Recycling is, once again, transformative. Just as it creates value out of seemingly useless materials, so too does it spread the gospel of environmentalism to cities and towns across the United Kingdom. On this occasion, there is some practicality to the proceedings. Recycling is not entirely mystified. But what connects Parley for the Oceans and *Hugh's War on Waste* is their shared unwillingness to directly confront the role of workers in the recycling industry. As though acknowledging the centrality of labour risks destabilising these narratives of creative, technological innovation, the human work of recycling, in both cases, is either ignored or casually dismissed. In each case, eliding the question of labour is a way of keeping sustainability and recycling both aesthetically and politically pure. Without a discussion of how the recycling industry relies on the same global divisions of labour as capitalism writ-large, the transformation of waste into upcycled luxury products can be conceived as an act of radical reimagination. This narrative around recycling functions on the erasure of human labour: an erasure necessary to sustain our fictions of sustainability.

*

In Shandong province, China, a young girl and her family live amongst piles of recyclable plastics. The small, makeshift recycling facility is also their place of work. Here, recyclables from the US and Europe are turned into plastic pellets that can then be sold on to a factory where plastic commodities are produced. The girl's name is Yi-Jie and she is one of the protagonists of Jiu-Liang Wang's 2016 documentary *Plastic China*. The scale of Wang's film is smaller, its gaze more microscopic, than the grand narratives of corporate environmentalism. There is no voiceover to guide viewers through the daily lives of recycling workers and their families. Wang's subjects rarely talk about the origins and destinations of the plastic within which they labour. Rather, they speak of their daily routines, and how they are shaped by their proximity to plastic. Women give birth in a field next to mounds of recyclables; children build toy computers from the waste, while their parents sit by archaic recycling machines through long winter days.

In Wang's documentary we learn about the lives of people who perform the very labour that is disavowed by corporate environmentalism. Here, recycling is no longer compressed within a single image of smooth transformation. *Plastic China* instead focuses on a single step in the recycling process, magnifying and extending one operation's impact on the workers tasked with producing the material that will later be turned into recycled commodities. The film fills in the gaps left by narratives of smooth integration. In an interview with the *New York Times*, Wang explains that his earlier interest in environmental degradation led him to a recycling facility in Oakland, California. It was there that he learned of the widespread practice of plastic waste exportation. Most plastic waste collected in the UK and the US is exported to regions in East Asia – Malaysia, Vietnam and Thailand are popular destinations – to be processed into new products. Until 2018, China was the main destination for plastic waste exported from Japan, Europe and the US. Once recyclables are exported, the nation of origin is absolved of any responsibility associated with their correct disposal. It is difficult to trace the journey of these exported plastics across the globe, though the findings of a recent investigative report by the *Guardian* indicate that recyclables often find their way to illegal dumping sites or are processed in unsafe conditions.

Everyone is constantly working. Throughout *Plastic China*, adults and children rake plastic waste, lift materials into machines or perform the acts of social reproduction, like cleaning and cooking, that are required to keep the workers and the business going. The machines of *Plastic China*'s recycling business are not sophisticated enough to make human labour superfluous. At one point, the owner of the facility, Kun, explains that he has found three tumours in his body. He refuses to see a doctor for fear that the diagnosis would be too devastating for his family. We learn that he blames his work for his ailments; the scene's subtitles read 'Damn plastics, my body is broken.' While recycled material can take on new lives, remoulded into useful new composites, recycling workers cannot be reconstituted and reborn in a different form. They only have one body, and the recycling industry has rendered that body most useful when it performs the work of cleaning and melting discarded plastics.

*

It's not difficult to find information about the recycling industry. There are government websites telling us how to recycle, industry newspapers that tell stories of expansion and consolidation, thinktank reports lamenting the high contamination rates of UK plastic waste. London City Hall's website informs us that the capital's residents do not recycle enough: the problem seems to be that there are too many blocks of flats in the city. Living in close quarters, stacked on top of each other, Londoners are not good for the environment. They discard all their waste in one bin, loath to expend energy on the trips up and down stairs that come with multiple coloured bags and separate collection days. Though some cities and local councils have implemented strict recycling policies, the London borough I live in separates garbage into only three bins: food waste, recyclables, and everything else. The practice of putting all recyclables – paper, plastics, cans, to name a few – into one bin is called single-stream recycling. It has its origins in 1990s California, but has since been adopted by local governments around the world. Advocates of single-stream recycling argue that the practice is less complicated than other recycling systems and therefore encourages more consumers to participate. Less room for error can also result in lower contamination rates, meaning that fewer items end up in bins where they don't belong.

Critics of single-stream recycling, however, are sceptical about the impact it can make. The recycling scholar Samantha MacBride, for instance, cites single-stream recycling as an example of 'busy-ness', defined in her 2011 book *Recycling Reconsidered* as 'a handy method of maintaining the status quo yet... simultaneously active, optimistic, and often makes people feel better.' 'Busy-ness' is an outcome of a recycling movement that holds 'contradictory positions', advocating for business interests and consumer freedoms at the same time as attempting to tackle the global problem of waste production and materials consumption. Plastics recycling has, for instance, been closely intertwined with the business interests of plastics companies who initially saw recycling as an opportunity to jump on the environmentalist bandwagon without limiting their productions. Enthused by the prospect of diversifying their operations by entering the recycling business, these companies soon recognised that recycling is too costly and inefficient to lead to significant profits. Local governments were left to shoulder the responsibility of continuing the scheme. Busy-ness, then, describes the state of an environmentalist practice that has always attempted to strike a balance between business interests and potential overall impact. It also captures the sense of optimism and self-satisfaction that we might feel when we place a plastic bottle or bag into a green bin with a label that reads 'Recycle, do the right thing.' With one simple gesture, the guilt of the initial purchase evaporates, giving way to a sense of righteousness and accomplishment.

Single-stream recycling is an effort to place as little responsibility as possible on consumers, leaving the actual labour of separating recyclable materials to waste management workers. In effect, the knowledge that our rubbish will undergo yet another sorting process encourages lacklustre recycling practices. It is 'busy-ness' at its finest, producing a good feeling of environmentalist activity whilst changing little about how the waste management industry functions as a whole. When items discarded in single-stream recycling facilities are removed from households they are transported to Materials Recovery Facilities (MRFs). Unlike their streamlined depiction in *Hugh's War on Waste*, MRFs are not places where plastics are turned into pellets and then, on the spot, remade into new products to be instantly redisseminated into the world. An MRF is a sorting facility, where sophisticated machinery separates different types of recyclable materials. One such facility stands in Bow, near East London's Lea Valley, and is owned by a company called Bywaters. The plant is a source of pride to the company, so much so that they gave a *Time Out London* reporter a tour of the facility in 2006. There was a lot to see. Piles and piles of waste that would one day become something newly useful. A hyper-efficient machine that is able to separate paper from plastic, glass from metals, through the use of lasers and aerodynamics.

You have to look closely to find evidence of workers and local residents in industry accounts. Information about the manual labour on which these facilities depend is, for instance, scattered only lightly throughout a report produced for the Waste and Resources Action Programme (WRAP) in 2006. Though the report gives detailed accounts and statistics about the work that takes place in MRFs around the UK, its language remains vague when it comes to the specific activities undertaken by the employees of a recycling company. There is talk of 'inspection stations' and 'quality control', 'residues' and 'contamination', all of which point to steps in the sorting process that can only be performed by human workers. The machine itself features more prominently, but it remains clear that no matter how sophisticated, no MRF can perform the work of separating materials without the help of manual human labour. Yet workers appear in WRAP's report in much the same way as they do in the facility itself. Their presence is acknowledged only as part of the machine they labour within, positioned throughout as a complement to the machine itself, there to ensure its continued functioning.

In a 2013 report of the UK Health and Safety Executive, recycling workers are more clearly identified as a part of the industry's narrative. This insight into the industry is damning. Here, readers are finally told of the dangers of exposure to bioaerosol and dust in MRFs. Workers complain of 'health problems [including] skin, respiratory, gastrointestinal and musculoskeletal symptoms and dexterity problems.' In most of the facilities surveyed for the report, few provisions were in place to protect workers from health risks. Of the 100 workers interviewed for the report, more than half were employed through agencies rather than directly by the recycling facility. Recycling work, it seems, is dangerous.

In June 2017, an unidentified employee of the Bywaters plant in Bow died whilst operating heavy machinery. In July 2016, Almamo Jammeh, Ousmane Diaby, Bangally Dukureh, Saibo Sillah and Muhamadou Jagana were crushed by a concrete structure at a recycling facility in Birmingham. This last case provides a rare, sobering glimpse into the lives of recycling workers. All five of the men who died in Birmingham came to the plant through a temporary work agency that promises its clients minimal paperwork and responsibility. Four of the five men were born in The Gambia, one in Senegal; all five had come to the UK from Spain. We learn about their lives only after their deaths because fictions of sophisticated machinery and responsible consumer behaviour render the labour involved in recycling invisible. Though the industry relies on such labour, it is consistently represented as supplemental rather than essential, temporary rather than permanent.

A workforce consisting largely of temporarily employed, poor, racialised labourers stands in stark contrast to recycling's public image as a harbinger of change. But recycling is an industry that exemplifies what theorist Michelle Yates refers to as environmentalism's refusal to recognise its continued production of 'the human-as-waste'. Whilst recycling turns material waste back into usable products, it reproduces hierarchies around class and race that turn human beings themselves into waste. By emphasising the role of the consumer and directing attention towards the achievements of technology, recycling distances itself from these existing hierarchies of subjugation. If there is no work, after all, there are also no mistreated workers who might tarnish the industry's environmentalist sheen. Recycling promises a tidy, neat future in which the loop of consumption and production is closed off, and neither waste nor the people who handle it exist. Recycling workers, who must correct the mistakes of consumer and machine, are uncomfortable evidence of the system's failures, and of sustainability's exploitative dimensions.

*

Recycling's detachment from waste management labour is not a new phenomenon. When recycling entered the political mainstream, as a result of a widely publicised scandal involving a 'garbage barge' which travelled around the country between January and July 1987 carrying 3,000 tonnes of New York trash, the concept immediately drew the attention of politically conservative dissenters. Libertarian columnist John Tierney's opinion piece 'Recycling is Garbage', published in June 1996, set a new record for hate-mail received by the *New York Times*. Tierney expressed shock that 'the citizens of the richest society in the history of the planet [had] suddenly [become] obsessed with personally handling their own waste', a task that he thought should be reserved for 'the most destitute members of society'. An assortment of dubious experiments, carried out by Tierney, led him to the conclusion that recycling was 'a waste of time and money, a waste of human and natural resources'. The overall cost of recycling drew most of Tierney's ire – why anyone would pay for the collection and transportation of recyclable waste, when it could just as easily and more cheaply go to a landfill in the US or abroad, was apparently beyond him. But it was the subject of who should do this labour that produced some of the piece's most hyperbolic claims. To prove a point about recycling's waste of human resources, Tierney asked a student at the University of Columbia to count every minute they dedicated to washing and sorting recyclable waste. Through some calculations involving both the time spent on recycling and the valuable pieces of New York City real estate taken up by recycling bins, Tierney deduced that his subject provided the equivalent of '$792 in home labour costs for each ton of bottles and cans collected' for free.

Tierney's piece contains little in the way of compelling critique. Its contribution lies instead in the strange inversions it perpetuates. Recycling, in Tierney's formulation, reconfigures actual and historical patterns of labour exploitation. Saying nothing about the histories of actually unfree and indentured, racialised labour on which the United States is built, Tierney goes so far as to make the sinister claim that recycling itself constitutes a type of 'forced labour'. In 'Recycling is Garbage', the practice of separating materials for future reprocessing is suspect because it asks people who are ordinarily shielded from contact with waste to perform work they consider beneath them. Tierney isn't lamenting the fact that recycling requires an outsized amount of additional labour, but that recycling assigns that labour to the wrong people. What is wasted, in Tierney's formulation, is the labour of educated US citizens.

Of course, decades of racial discrimination and labour exploitation have long ensured that someone with the background of Tierney's test subject need not worry about performing unpaid or unwaged work. Though recycling purports to shift some of the work involved in waste management on to consumers, recycling facilities are still largely reliant on a workforce that consists of poor, often migrant workers. The recycling industry continues many of the discriminatory practices on which the broader waste industry relies. Recycling facilities are disproportionately located in low-income areas. Conditions in these facilities range from unhygienic to outright hazardous. Because consumers are under-informed about which materials are suitable for recycling, the workers who handle reusable waste encounter old newspapers and yoghurt containers alongside sharp metals and biological waste, the latter of which may have to be manually removed. In one case recorded by the *Economist*, an owner of a recycling facility in North Carolina complained that his employees had found a six-foot shark among the contents of a recycling bin.

The groundbreaking 1987 report *Toxic Wastes and Race*, published in the United States, identified over-exposure to environmental hazards as a central tenet of environmental racism; a study conducted on the report's twentieth anniversary, under the direction of environmental justice pioneer Robert Bullard, found that this situation persists and has, in some cases, worsened. Twelve years after this second study, the populations of East Los Angeles and Flint, Michigan, are still reeling from the effects of lead poisoning on their communities. In LA, airborne lead particles from a nearby car battery recycling plant contaminated soil in predominantly Latino neighbourhoods nearby. In Flint, a mismanaged change in water supply to the majority black city resulted in contaminated drinking water. These historic and ongoing structures of environmental injustice frame Tierney's panic over the possibility that recycling could put middle-class, white populations in close proximity to waste. The reality is that under a political and economic regime that is closely aligned with racism and capitalism, this will never be the case.

*

With its insistence that free markets need not be affected by efforts to combat environmental degradation, recycling's trajectory from utopian promise to uneasy compromise makes it a uniquely late liberal form of waste management. Recycling promises more than a world without waste; it supports a fiction of sustainable and endless growth, economic and otherwise. The recuperative gestures of environmentalist visionaries are therefore as much about sustaining the environment as they are a means of justifying the continuation of the economic and political projects that have resulted in large-scale environmental crisis. Mary Douglas's famous 1966 description of dirt as 'matter out of place' has given way to the notion – now widely accepted – that recyclables, when handled correctly, contain the potential for broader societal renewal. Recyclable waste is distinctly *in* place as a component of a broader, productive culture of green capitalism that makes environmentalism commensurable with continued consumption. In perpetuating the idea that radical change can take place without a radical ideological shift, recycling supplants the labour of sustainability on to a global underclass, all the while insisting that consumers are making a significant contribution to environmentalist causes. Recycling relies on global hierarchies of difference that make labour exploitation possible. The logic that recycling perpetuates extends beyond the bounds of environmentalism. It is a logic of sustainability, not just for the planet but for the political and economic systems that govern it.

Yet, in spite of their failings, both recycling and the wider culture of capitalist environmentalism continue. The US brewery conglomerate Constellation Brands – which produces Mexican beers such as Corona and Modelo for export only – has recently been embroiled in a PR battle with local activists after the company announced its plans for a mega-brewery in Baja California, Mexico, that would severely deplete local drinking water reserves. Though Corona purportedly cares for the waters near which its beers are consumed, the company does not extend that same care to water reserves further inland. Ocean Cleanup's plastic collection device, Wilson, spent less than six months in the Pacific before it broke and had to be returned to California for repairs. The charity insists that their next attempt at removing plastics from the ocean through technological innovation will succeed. In 2017, the Chinese government announced restrictions on foreign waste imports. Largely understood as a populist gesture, the repercussions of this policy shift reverberated around the world. Because people were largely unaware of where their recycling went, recyclers continued to separate their waste unperturbed by events that had rocked the global recycling industry. Soon, plastic began to pile up in recycling centres around California until it had to be dumped into landfills. One outcome of the Chinese import restrictions is that plastic waste is now being exported to other destinations in East Asia. Crisis has not led to a shift in business practice.

As long as recycling remains primarily an industry, rather than one component of a popular political push for environmental justice, it will continue to replicate already existing inequalities while doing little to facilitate a more sustainable way of life. If sustainability is to be more than a means of maintaining the status quo, its advocates need to embrace a broader definition of environmental justice, one that extends beyond nature to include people. This environmental justice should be based on the demands made by indigenous, colonised and racialised activists around the globe. Land must be redistributed, accumulation has to end, labour exploitation must cease; in short, there can be no environmentalism under capitalism and there can be no environmental justice without racial justice. The goal of environmentalist actions cannot be the continuation of systems that rely on exploitation, dispossession, and racial hierarchies. Real environmentalism must be divested from ideologies of regeneration. Fighting against the condition of waste and wasting requires a different call to action; not to renew but to revolt.

FROM MULLAE

KANG YOUNG-SOOK
tr. JANET HONG

The car reeked of chocolate. The forty-something man ate it every waking moment, turning all that he touched sweet and sticky. My job was to remove the chocolate traces he left behind with a wet wipe. I didn't mind. After all, he was my man.

From time to time, dreary buildings with an obscure purpose popped up on either side of the road. The forest was mostly brown. I didn't want to leave the city. The scene we passed through reminded me of deserted blocks you'd see in a horror movie, like Lego buildings with gaping toothless mouths. We entered District Y and continued on the country road for about ten minutes before we finally stopped. I recalled seeing a half-faded name on the top part of an apartment building.

'Isn't that it? Did you see it?' he cried, as if to himself.

He put the car in reverse and turned off the engine. To our right, an apartment building called Bluebird something-or-other jutted from a field at an unnatural angle. He yanked up the hand brake, and I pulled out another wet wipe to erase the chocolate he'd smeared on it.

It was three months ago. We had stopped around here and squinted through the car window, like settlers newly arrived on the frontier. The twelve-storey building was erected on a bare field, which started hardly a hundred metres from the road. There was no fence, not even a low wall, and no other facilities, like a children's playground slide. The frozen patches of snow, drilled into the ground like so many dots, and the swish of the whirling wind – these were the only things I registered. Behind the apartment several paddy fields stretched to the hills, and from that point the land was all farmland. Frequent billboards displaying cartoon images of cows let you know you'd entered an agricultural zone.

As soon as I opened the window, an acrid tang, difficult to describe, like the smell of rain hitting the scorched earth, surged into my throat. He twisted around in his seat, looking for his cigarettes. I followed him out of the car. While I narrowed my eyes and peered about me, the stench kept burrowing into my body. It smelled like baked dust, clammy metal, a polluted river.

He smoked, leaning against the driver's side window. I stepped off the sidewalk on to the field and walked towards the apartment. The winter sun was blinding. I stared up at the balconies that faced the road. White sheets flapped in the wind, and I heard a door open and shut, and someone's hacking cough. But I'd only imagined these things; in truth, I neither saw nor heard anything.

'Let's go wait in the car!' he cried, waving his hand.

I turned up my collar against the cold. Freight trucks barrelled past, kicking up dust. I finally identified the oppressive smell that hung in the air. It was death. The same smell I'd detected in the middle of the room when I was young, that frightening smell I'd been forced to accept.

'This is the perfect place for you. You can have a fresh cup of milk every morning. You'll get better in no time. Happy? Why shouldn't you be?'

With a hand sheathed in a leather glove, he pointed at the billboard of cows on the side of the road and patted my shoulder. R wouldn't stop at milk. He'd bring me a whole cow, if he thought it'd be good for me. The ground beneath us started vibrating just then and a military truck as big as a tank came charging down the road. We got back in the car, shivering from the cold. The paddy fields behind the apartment had grown dark already. An hour had gone by, but there was still no sign of the estate agent.

'Where the hell is he?'

Several times, R picked up his cell phone and flung it down.

'You sure he's coming?' I asked. 'Did you talk to him? Maybe he forgot.'

He dozed, arms crossed over his chest. Big snowflakes fell on the windshield. Without thinking, I leaned forward and opened my mouth. I must have been very thirsty. Right then two children sprang out from the east entrance of the apartment. Both were wearing long padded jackets and surgical masks decorated with animal faces. Holding hands, they walked across the field and stepped on to the sidewalk. They glanced at us as they walked past. After a few steps, the smaller child looked back once more. I raised my hand in an awkward wave. Ignoring me, they quickly walked along the narrow road, still holding hands. Each time trucks roared closely past them, I couldn't help but hold my breath.

*

Our last day in Mullae was exhausting. To be honest, I had zero expectations about District Y, where we were moving for my husband's work. We'd been comfortable in Mullae, a dark and dingy neighbourhood, once home to many textile mills. When the mills added *Inc.* to their names and moved into office buildings, the alleys were overtaken by small-scale ironworks and the smell of machine grease. The snowbanks piled on street corners were always dirty and the last on earth to dissolve. All the dust in Seoul seemed to collect in Mullae.

I don't know at what point artists started to gather between Mullae Station and Yeongdeungpo Station, driven out from the pricier side of the Han River. While many metal fabrication and welding shops still remained, vacant work-shops received fresh coats of paint and were turned into art studios. Flowers emblazoned on a shop door. Characters in a mural. For some strange reason, these splashes of colour suited the grey neighbourhood. Early in the morning, it was the industrial workers who strode along the alleys. Not that the artists came out at night. Most of the time they stayed in their studios. Sometimes, though, they came out for a late-night drink, and could be seen sitting at a table next to the ironworkers.

Where these two most opposite groups in the world came together was Boksun's Place. With a large sunflower adorning its sign, it was the only nice restaurant in Mullae. The ironworkers weren't a talkative bunch. For the first hour, all they did was consume the liquor and meat before them, heads tilted towards the table at similar angles. They ate and drank until their foreheads shone with grease, oblivious to the fact that their mouths were ringed with soot. At last, when their bellies were full, they began to talk about their days. Though they tended to be crude and vulgar, they never bothered anybody else.

At the next table, artists with long hair and bright clothes smoked and drank soju while they ate. They were just as quiet as the ironworkers, but possessed a lively energy. After sitting in such proximity to the young artists, I loved walking out of the restaurant at the end of the night and seeing the grey sky flushing red in the distance. With hardly any streetlights, the streets turned dark around seven o'clock, but still I shivered from happiness.

There was a girl. She went in and out of the restaurant kitchen, helping the owner trim soybean sprouts and sometimes even grabbing beer and soju from the cooler for the customers. She smoked freely with the factory men nearly double her age, not thinking twice about borrowing their lighters. But whenever anyone said or did something she didn't like, she flew into a rage and screamed, 'I'm an artist, goddamn it, a frigging painter!' The other artists then filled their shot glasses with soju and drank to her, crying, 'Yup, you're the best, bravo!' The ironworkers, however, cast their gazes to the floor with sheepish smiles, or tipped back their shot glasses with no change in their expressions.

I would come across her suddenly in various parts of the neighbourhood. There she would be at Boksun's Place, at the public bath, in front of the produce truck, or on Rodeo Street – there was always a Rodeo Street or a Rodeo Karaoke in every lousy city I'd ever lived in. Her hair was styled differently each time: in pigtails that hung down past her collarbone, or twisted up in a topknot, or strewn loose across her shoulders. Still I recognised her instantly; she possessed an unusual, restless energy and never stopped moving, not even for a second. I'd thought I would run into her at least once before we moved to District Y, but I didn't.

The first time I ever saw her was at a supermarket check-out. Before the clerk had finished tallying up her bill, she had wandered over to another aisle to browse through other items. 'Excuse me, Ms XXX, could you sign here please?'

I couldn't help but smile. We had the exact same name. How could such a pretty girl have the same name as me and also live in Mullae? I clasped my hands together out of sheer happiness. It made me want to stop anyone I came across and shake their hand.

She signed the card reader and smoothed down her frizzy hair. After she thanked the clerk in a ringing voice, she clomped out of the store in ankle boots and purple pants. I followed her out. With a plastic bag in hand, she headed to Boksun's Place. Seated between the other young artists, she looked five, no, ten years younger than me. Soon afterwards, my husband and his colleagues came into the restaurant as if we'd arranged to meet there. One of the other artists unwrapped a muffler from around his neck and put it around the girl's shoulders. She and her friends kept snickering, while eating kimchi stew and drinking soju. Then she glanced at me.

Though I wanted to gaze back at her, I quickly turned away. A short while later, I looked at her out of the corner of my eye. Maybe I'd only imagined it, but I was sure she'd gazed at me. She was beautiful, but odd, constantly placing kisses on her friends' noses. For some reason, my belly grew warm whenever I watched her. An artist with my name, and a painter!

On our last evening in Mullae, my husband and I ate dinner with his co-workers at Boksun's Place. As we walked home, people left us one by one for the bus stop or their alleys, until the only people left were me, my husband, and an older bachelor of whom my husband was especially fond. He was a large man; he kept throwing his arms around my husband in a bear hug.

'Ah, bro, come on now, bro,' my husband said over and over again, as he hugged the older man's head to his chest and placed a kiss on top. He slung his arm around the man's shoulders.

Such strange men. I stood off to the side like a streetlight, watching the clumsy affection between the two lumbering men, and followed at a distance when they started off again.

Soon we arrived at the older man's house. The two men embraced each other once more. Just then noise filled the dark alley. The young artists passed by the opening, and I saw a flash of purple pants. It was the girl! But the group disappeared just as quickly.

When I reached out to slip my arm through my husband's, he put his arm around my shoulders. The neighbourhood was quite dangerous, but I wasn't afraid when he was with me.

As soon as we opened the gate to our multi-unit, the sensor light on the first floor came on, shutting off when the light on the second floor switched on. I gazed down at the alley until everything went dark again. I looked and looked, but saw no one. After I'd helped my husband lie down and pulled off his socks for him, I headed back out. I'd never walked the alley alone, but I wasn't scared.

I rushed out on to the main street and crossed the road as if I needed to meet someone urgently. I seemed to have gone a little crazy. I headed for the five-way intersection where all the artists' studios were located. I hurried along the slippery streets. The ironworks nearby had closed hours earlier. Though the men sometimes put up plastic sheets and worked well into the night, most of the industrial shops were shuttered and the interiors pitch black. I strode into an alley and stopped at a studio that still had its light on, nestled in between the dark workshops. I stood on tiptoe and peered into its tinted window. I saw the girl. I had found her.

The back of her head looked small and her hands extremely big. The table was cluttered with every kind of liquor bottle, from wine to soju to beer, and her enormous canvas was unspeakably dark. Behind the easel, paintings lined the wall, but I didn't have a clue what they were about. A headless, legless torso from which a giant eye stared. A figure hovering in the air, the head separated from the body. There was one painting that was completely black. The girl sat in a corner, staring blankly at the canvases or down at her phone.

My God, I found myself trying to go inside! Luckily, the door was locked. Even though her paintings were so frightening, I didn't have a nightmare that night. I'd never told anyone how I used to get down on my knees every night and pray I wouldn't have a scary dream. That's the kind of fool I was, but whenever I thought about the girl, I grew calm and meek, just like a tame animal.

*

The estate agent knocked on the car window with a leather-gloved hand. Only then did I see his old Sonata parked behind us.

'Everyone dreams of this country life,' he said as he removed his knitted hat. He seemed to smirk, pointing at the billboard where cows flashed massive udders and human-looking smiles. 'Now you can have a fresh cup of milk every morning.'

It was something I'd heard many times. I kept my sunglasses on, half-listening. I wasn't ready to accept the fact that we were a long way from Mullae.

As soon as we entered the suite, the agent fished out a bundle of newspaper from his plastic bag and started to fan out the pages on the floor until the entire space was covered. The apartment got a lot of light and had a comfortable feel, apart from the noise of the traffic outside. The agent said the place would look cosy once the furniture came in. As he circled the living room, he said all the typical things that estate agents say.

I opened the kitchen window that looked out on to the paddy fields in the back. I liked the way they stretched all the way to the hills.

'We'll take it.'

The estate agent gave a wide smile and awkwardly opened his arms. 'Why don't we head to the office then?'

My husband stepped out of the bathroom and said with a laugh that he'd do as I wished. The estate agent walked toward the front door. I followed him to the entrance and turned, gazing at the newspaper laid out on the floor. The agent had left red footprints wherever he'd stepped. It was blood.

But with nowhere else to go, we had no choice but to move in.

The shouts of children woke me in the morning. I opened the front door, but the hallway was quiet. Sunlight streamed in through the windows. It was too cold to open the large living-room window, so I opened the small window above the kitchen sink. Children stood in a ring, staring down at something. Black objects both big and small dotted the frozen paddy fields.

'They're dead!' the children shouted. 'The birds are all dead!'

I squeezed my eyes shut. Dead birds littered the white fields. I put on a sweater and slid the big window open. The cold wind rushed in. There was a black feather stuck in the frame. The second I reached through the open window, it blew in and stuck to my chest.

Why had so many birds died here? It was difficult for someone like me to understand. Truly, I didn't know a thing; I couldn't even begin to guess the cause. I had to tell my husband about the dead birds, I had so much to tell him, but he didn't return. All day I watched the news and ate peanuts. District Y wasn't the only place to experience mass bird deaths. There were reports of mass bird deaths all over the country. The reason was unclear. Experts speculated that trauma, bad weather, or the noise from local fireworks was to blame.

My husband returned close to midnight. He looked noticeably thinner. I clasped his face in my hands, but he didn't crack a smile. He'd always brought back news from the outside world. I believed everything he said. After all, I was frail and he was strong; I knew nothing and he knew everything. I lay down with my head in his lap.

'There was blood in the valley stream,' he said. 'It was all frozen and snow was falling on top.'

The smell of blood bothered me. I pushed my head between his legs. I put my nose to his jacket and sniffed the fishy, copper stink. He stroked my face and hair with his broad hand.

'I have to head out early in the morning. I just want to go to bed.'

He looked exhausted. He cried out several times in his sleep.

*

I heard the hairdryer, and the cabinet door open and shut.

'Don't go outside. It's supposed to be freezing today,' my husband said to me while I was still half-asleep. Soon after, I heard the front door close.

Cold mornings are unbearable for those with low blood pressure. I could barely lift my head and place my feet on the floor. Luckily, I didn't collapse back on to the bed. I opened the curtains and window, and sniffed the wind blowing in from the paddy fields. The news was going on about the mass bird deaths again. Several hundreds of dead birds had fallen from the sky in downtown Hong Kong, and about five hundred had died in a small Japanese village due to a sudden cold spell. All over the world thousands of birds had been found dead, in the southern part of the United States, Finland, and Sweden.

Every morning the milkman placed a glass bottle of organic milk outside my door, but there were no deliveries that day. I discovered a thick feather in the frame of the small corridor window, which looked out on to the back paddies. I took it inside and stuck it in the empty milk bottle where I had placed the feather from the other day.

My husband was still not home past midnight. I finally fell asleep. When I woke in the middle of the night and climbed out of bed, I discovered him in the living room. He was sitting on the floor and drinking soju, illuminated by just a small lamp. My husband – a large man – looked strangely small. I sat behind him and started massaging his back. His shoulders were stiff and tense.

'Did you wash up?'

He shook his head.

'Did you run into an old lover then?'

He shook his head once more.

'Isn't it dark? Should I turn on the light?' I said, pretending to be cheerful. 'You really need to wash. You smell bad.'

He got to his feet and headed to the bathroom. I caught another whiff of the stench from where he'd been sitting.

I went into the bathroom after he came out. The floor by the bathtub looked a bit red. I brushed a finger along the tiles. A film of oil came off on my finger. Strands of his hair were caught in the sink. But the stench overpowered everything. I broke out in goosebumps again.

In bed I stroked his back. He was still awake.

'Can you hold me for a bit?' I asked.

He turned and put his arms around me. He still smelled of blood.

'Promise me you won't go outside,' he said, as if I were a child. He held me tightly, tucking my head under his chin. 'It freaks me out to be a human walking around on two legs.'

All night I slipped in and out of nightmares. It was hard to bear the noise from the suite upstairs. Anyone would have assumed an important football match was on. The toilet flushed, a woman screamed, a man swore. I lay with the blanket pulled over my face, clutching the edge of the fabric. When the fight upstairs finally ended, I heard snoring. The woman kept crying. In the end, I must have fallen asleep, because her crying seeped into my dreams. I tore open the ceiling and climbed up. Light shone through the crack in the bathroom door. When I pushed the door open, I saw the woman hunched over on the toilet, weeping. I stroked her hair and begged, 'Please, could you stop crying? My bed is right below and I can't sleep.'

When she raised her face at last, it was the girl from Mullae. The strength left my legs, and I sank to the bathroom floor.

I kept wandering in and out of the girl's paintings. When I was gazing at a painting of a horse's severed head, my foot seemed to fall in and then my arm, until my face was touching the severed head. But there was no blood, and the horse didn't make a sound. Did this mean something had happened to the girl? I hoped she was okay.

In the morning, I braced myself and stepped outside. The sun shone brightly, but the wind was fierce. There were three tents set up in the vacant lot opposite the apartment. They hadn't been there a few days earlier. I crossed the street to have a look. A woman in black stood in front of the tents, holding a bundle of pamphlets.

'Ma'am, you've got to read this! Don't just stand there, come and have a look.

This district has become a place of death. You need to get out of here. Just forget everything and go!'

The woman in black tried to come closer. I was scared of her dark eyebrows. I dodged the speeding cars and managed to make it across. By the apartment entrance, young children were poking a dead bird with sticks, and middle-school boys were standing around smoking. The pamphlets that had blown in from the tents flapped madly as they sailed toward the field.

I strode around the building and stumbled into the paddy fields. I stared at the farms in the distance; I didn't think I could make it all the way there in my condition. Still I set out blindly; I needed to know what was happening. My feet sank into the mud that hadn't frozen over. Each time I passed over a ridge, I looked back at the apartment growing smaller and smaller like a scale model. When I got closer to the hills, I heard a different noise. I was scared. If I crossed one more ridge, I would be at the brow, which was the entrance point to the farms. Right then trucks started to file out on to the unpaved road from the agricultural zone. The air was thick with the smell of pigs. Terrified, I pressed the speed dial on my phone without thinking. My husband didn't pick up.

The soles of my shoes were filthy. Before I went back into the apartment building, I found an outdoor tap in the back beside the bins. Luckily it wasn't frozen. As soon as I twisted the tap, icy water gushed out. The water that washed off my shoes on to the patch of cement was red. I dropped the rubber hose and raced toward the entrance. The kids who had been smoking were still there. I stood next to them, panting.

'Let's go kill a dog, too,' they said, flicking away their cigarette butts.

My husband returned around midnight with two bottles of soju.

'Why not just buy them by the box?' I said. I stroked his cheek. 'You've been drinking every night since we moved here.'

He let out a heavy sigh and started to say something.

'No. Don't tell me what's happening out there.'

As if he understood, he stretched out his legs and lay me down on the floor next to him. 'I can't remember the last time I held my wife. How about we do a little something tonight?'

The dark living room would light up whenever a car would pass by, shining its headlights into the window, and fall dark once more. I twisted around and gazed at his face. Unbuttoning his pants with one hand, I brought my mouth down between his legs. There was the smell of blood again. I pushed up his shirt with one hand and fumbled for his penis. I couldn't find it. The window lit up and grew dark, repeatedly, at greater and greater intervals.

'Don't tell me anything,' I said, looking up at his face. 'I don't want to know.'

*

The next morning, there was a knock at the door. I finally answered it after the doorbell had rung several times. Smiling women were gripping pamphlets, their faces raw and red from the cold. They had come from an animal protection group. I found it difficult to listen to what they had to say and gazed towards the window the entire time. I kept licking the roof of my mouth; it felt as if something was starting to bud on the tip of my tongue. I hardly budged all day. I sat in the same spot on the living-room floor, and took down and put back the objects that were within arm's reach. I even flipped through our wedding album. When I'd first told my friends that I was getting married, they had opened their eyes wide and waved their hands in front of their faces.

'Don't do it! He's going to eat you up!' a friend had said. 'How can you marry someone with a face like that?'

Still I tried to convince them that he was a good, caring man, and not some barbaric animal as they thought, but they didn't believe me. He really was a good, caring man.

Then for some reason, after we were married, my body started to break down.

My husband's relatives, who'd always told me they liked me because I was so strong and robust, now asked what the matter was each time we met. My husband had expected to fill the house with a brood of boys who took after him; he'd believed they would be his ticket to retirement. I sensed his disappointment, even though he never voiced anything of that sort.

Strictly speaking, it wasn't my fault. I liked the fact it was just us two. There were too many cars, the Arctic glaciers were melting at an alarming rate, buildings were constantly collapsing, wars were breaking out everywhere, and the world was full of cancer patients – the last thing I wanted to do was leave behind children in this world. I had no desire to keep even a dog or cat as a pet. My resolve never wavered. After all, I had my husband to keep me company.

I heard the key in the door. My husband staggered into the apartment looking sloppy and bedraggled, as if he'd been in a steam room until just now. His entire body was wet. He sank to his knees and fell forward on his face.

'Bad day?'

I could hardly talk because of the canker sore.

He lay motionless, his cheek stuck to the living-room floor. I removed his shoes and socks. His insoles were wet. The hairs on my arms stood up, and my face stung as if the skin had grown too tight. My taste buds seemed to swell more and more until they filled my mouth.

He didn't want to eat. He couldn't because of the nausea. He crawled to the bed, and I filled a small plastic basin with water, and washed his face and hands. All evening he burned up with a high fever. He kept moaning, and would sit up all of a sudden as if he were going to vomit, and then lie down again. Many times, I wetted a towel with cold water and placed it on his head. I nearly forgot about my canker sore.

He woke in the middle of the night. I found him in his longjohns in the living room, eating a chocolate bar. He looked fine, but something in his expression made him appear strange and rather simple. We sat side by side with our shoulders touching and ate chocolate non-stop. We ate until the smell of chocolate overpowered everything and our heads went numb.

There was a commotion across the street. The women in black were by the tents again. Things turned clamorous whenever they appeared. They'd been there since morning, holding signs that screamed: *The world ended in the 60s!*

Therefore, the world had ended before I was even born. In District Y alone, 2,000 pigs had been slaughtered. It was a number I couldn't fathom.

'Shame on you, wicked officials, for slaughtering pigs without compensating farmers!'

I shook my head. I didn't want to listen to the voice on the speakers.

The middle-school boys who had huddled by the apartment entrance now smoked across the street by the tents. Right then I saw a procession of trucks come out from the farms. There were over ten trucks. Covered with black tarp, they sped down the dirt lane, leaving behind a strange smell. I wanted to know what would heal my tongue. It felt as if it would start bleeding, but I had no choice but to bear it. The canker sore, the stench, the voice coming through the speakers – they were all too much to bear.

The next day, my husband left early for work.

'Don't go outside.'

He spoke as if he were making a vow.

In the afternoon, I got into our old car and sped along the road where the trucks packed with pigs had gone. Government agents in masks and white plastic suits stood at the entrance to the hills, controlling access into the area. Regular traffic was not permitted to enter. They told me to turn back immediately. I couldn't hear what they said. All they did was wave their batons in the air. My tongue hurt, and I was terrified.

'I'm supposed to meet my husband,' I said. 'He works here. He asked me to bring him something.'

But they just shook their heads at me. I saw the sun starting to fall behind the hills.

'I'll stop here then. I won't go in. I'll wait for him here, I promise!'

I parked the car on the side of the road and sat inside for a long time. About an hour later, when their shift ended, the agents got in a car and drove off.

There was a valley to my left. I walked up the steep dirt lane marked by numerous tyre tracks. I hadn't climbed very far when the hill levelled out abruptly and I saw a strange sight. It was a giant pit, with an enormous mound swelling up from it, a mound endlessly vast and wide, like a vessel from outer space. Empty trucks surrounded the bulge, and people in masks and white plastic suits were pulling a massive canvas sheet over it – no, it was closer to a white foil tarp. They grabbed the edge of the tarp, dragged it to the centre, and walked up to the opposite rim. Trucks rumbled past constantly, and I heard shrill whistles and the crackling of walkie-talkie radios. I didn't see my husband. From all around the pit, the white suits grabbed the edge of the tarp and dragged it over to the centre and walked back to the rim. A little while later, everything grew chaotic as they marched in and out of the pit. I pictured all the pig carcasses inside. The vast pile of carcasses rotting and disintegrating inside the pit.

The sun was falling unbelievably fast. I couldn't find my husband. Steam rose from the white mound. Agents in plastic suits kept tugging the tarp over the bulge. Nausea welled up in me. I wondered if this is what morning sickness felt like. *See? What a pain*, I mumbled. *Thank God I'm not pregnant.*

I needed to go home. I looked around before heading down to the car. The hills were growing dark at an alarming rate, and the lights down by the road were starting to come on one by one. The pit was darkening, too. I was about to make my way down the hill when I glanced back. Then in that unhappy moment I saw her – the girl from Mullae.

In purple pants, with her long hair streaming behind her, she dashed over the white mound of entangled carcasses. She swung her arms like an action painter, like a small insect dancing. All I could do was stand rooted in the same spot and watch. Darkness fell over District Y. When I could no longer see the pit or the girl, I stumbled down the hill.

I turned on the engine and started to drive. The car was almost out of petrol. There was nowhere left to go. I crawled along the dirt lane. Up ahead, I saw a disinfection checkpoint. When had they set it up? The cars in front of me slowed down. A lighted sign warned that all vehicles exiting infected premises must undergo decontamination.

I hoped the fumes of slaughter rising from the pit would not reach Mullae. I hoped the blood spilling into the soil from the pit would not reach the girl.

The car ahead was finished. It was my turn. All of a sudden, I missed my husband. I wanted to tell him now was the time – now, more than ever – for us to love each other. I kept looking back to see if his car was coming. At that very moment, sprayers began to blast my car with chemicals.

KAYE DONACHIE

Based upon writers, artists and characters from works of fiction, Kaye Donachie's oil on linen paintings are a high modern fantasy of female beauty and intelligence. Her portraits are swoon triggers, executed in the register of devotion, romance, ache. Like visions that evaporate soon after waking, each has an ephemeral quality. Soon, it seems, the woman upon whom you are gazing will disappear into the blue of night, or dissolve into the backs of your eyelids.

Donachie's 2014 exhibition at Maureen Paley, London was inspired by the protagonist of Marguerite Duras's novel *The Malady of Death* (1982) – a doomed narrative in which a woman is hired to live with a man by the sea and teach him how to love. More recent paintings gesture towards the poet Iris Tree, and the characters in Ann Quin's novel *Three* (1966) – a story of a couple coming to terms with the death of a younger woman who enters their relationship.

While they take their cue from pre-existing characters from history or literature, Donachie's portraits are only ever loosely moored to any given life; viewed *en masse*, they could be many faces of the same reverie. Her paintings speak to a wider interest in biography, and the fecund territory that overlaps remembrance and invention. The continued popularity of historical biography is due in part, perhaps, to the freedom the dead give to the living – freedom to shape new stories and scenarios from what is left behind, as if the details of a life are a palette of paint ready to be moved into new expressions.

In addition to portraiture, Donachie also produces paintings and cyanotype prints that occupy the interstice between still-life and landscape. A form of rudimental photography developed in the nineteenth century and popularised by the Victorian botany enthusiast Anna Atkins, the cyanotype is recognisable for its rich blue colouration. Donachie uses the method to produce vignettes in which waves lap against flowers, orbs and elegantly poised hands: a distillation of the mood and style of the women who occupy her canvases.

PLATES

XXIII

CYANOTYPES

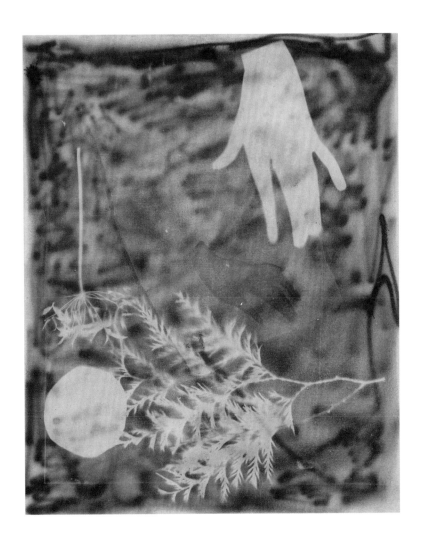

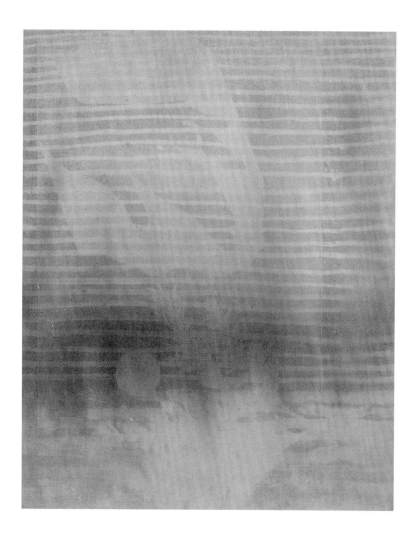

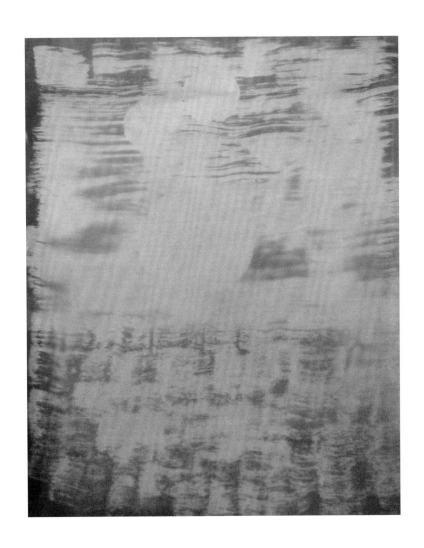

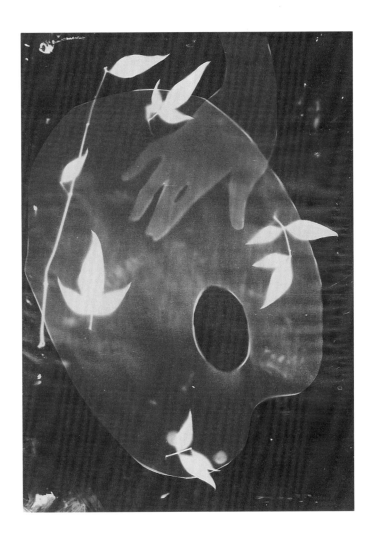

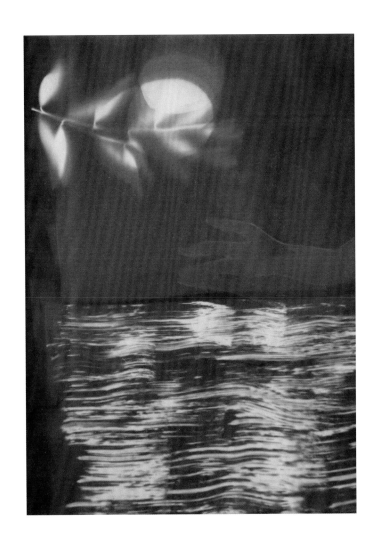

XXIV

SO MAYER

POETRY

PALATE

'If you can mak't apparent
That you have tasted her in Bed'
William Shakespeare, *Cymbeline*, II.iv.57

Swete

      In tendere touchinge of þing, & tastinge of swete
          squete spiceri to tast & smelle
                spoon sweets :: sweet spot
                where sweatspicy to the taste
        keep a spicery of you tapped & packed
      a tender touch to sweaten a dish

Salt Lick

We fucked the restaurants shut, exchanging
eucharist, eucharist between our lips &
their echoes   oh a cunt
architecture: acousmatic perfect
amphitheatrical resonance reverb   erating

this wave pull is labial, the self
some shelving-off. Such tumbling
to find itself just/here. holding
at the suck &

in the heat I like a salt-lick

silicate   holy cairn
at cavemouth
lost beneath the waves that long & rustle
on return

Mara

call me
      she said
          oh naomi
          call me
       Mara   [salt of this sea
for life

[with
out
you]
is
bit
ter

Musk

how you are unafraid   in the starlit
armpit   spelunking freestyle &
tell me you like musk not
marble   longhairs
European-style   what gets
caught in yr bright white teeth
the cat   of it I get you
civety   scent-trailed   you call it little snail
my shell and its antenna'd head
deepsafe hadron spin   no bars held

Umami

If... Mrs S. has any taste she will oblige me by sending me
half a yard, no matter of what color, so it be not black.

sub   liminal a kind of ribbon
used for edge-binding   profound
fingerwork   neat yr basting

gets deeper gets   squidinky
skins skin for the fat & crackle
overunder crura go on for ½ a

yard :: zone :: asphalt texture
or gravel, ribbon, rubber   granular
at play micro & that atom-shift thing

so it be (not)
so it be ~~not~~
so it be

TEACUP

'The derivative porcellana [from *porcus*, pig, used in nursery language as a word for vulva, according to Varro] survives in Romance (Fr. *porcelaine*, It. *porcellana*) as a designation for a type of shell which had the shape of the female external pudenda.'
J. N. Adams, *The Latin Sexual Vocabulary*

Pink pink like the. Everything. Rose light falling on her rows
of precisely-chipped white in the pop-up gallery window. I have to stop casting
teacups she says to T (for tired, for -count
down). Tiresias toasts her with their mug; favourite London thing,
the breakfasts. The old café at Smithfields, early morning, sneaking
non-vegan. What if, thinks Medusa, seeing a spill of thick-
walled builder's tea mugs linked by clay sausages, fat fingers a
chain saying *empire*, saying all the tea in the warehouse on the quay,
Tobacco Docks where London marks colonialism with haute
shopping. Second time as Amex, right? Read the leaves: it's
referendum day and M is packing. Her little teacup pig, her handbag
dog. A pet to pet, she thinks of it to stop herself – themself, y/n – thinking
of it. T's gift from their last trip (to, is it?) home. Adjusts
her cord bags as they walk through the city swagged humid-heavy
sweating, already, towards rain. There is a distinction
thinks M between hard-paste and soft-paste porcelain and it is temp
erature. Yes / No. Stickers everywhere: leave remain love EU reclaim.
Two brown-skinned creatures under the English sun, tender
as the traces of rivers beneath the city. She can feel them
in her feet, fleet. T talks tea, they are writing about the rise,
artisanal, about the looseness of loose leaf, shifted from art criticism
to something. Percolating. Starting with an artist who paints with tea.
Maps. Plantations. Hill stations. Displacements. Water crises. Unhappy
valleys of national addiction. *Spilt, milk* their show is called. M wanted
to call her chipped teacup piece *White Tears* but the gallery poo-poo'd.
Where are they walking? Along the Thames, like Katharine Hilbery dis-
engaged in Woolf's *Night and Day*. They talk about Orlando
matamoros, Woolf's Orientalist hero, furios@, swinging his sword
at (ouch) a Moor's head. Page one. And in the film, the Khan (played by Québecois Jesus
Lothaire Bluteau) notes the English have a habit of collecting
countries. Count, cunt. Enjambment enunciates both ways. Here, they realise,
the Leave/Remain flotillas crossed paths in a watery joust. *We want
our waters back*. Well you still sing Rule Britannia, not you *porcellana*
but – They, she (they?) replies, them. As in: the other side of us. Not you they. Them-they
they sing *rules the waves*. Rhymes with, says T, as they reach Tate
Modern, that sugar rush monument to plantation wealth. *WHEREISANAMENDIETA*

the day before the riverboat pantomime. Sublime > ridiculous. The life of a city
should always be in uproar, says T, leaning on the Millennium Bridge.
This also has been one of the dark places of the earth, she says back,
A-Level English giving her the(ir) words for it. Here where the beautiful artist-protestors
crossed, red-handed. *STOP GLAMOURISING VIOLENT MEN*
their sign read. Look west, to the Hayward, where they'd seen
the Mendieta show three years ago, T re-appearing out of the blue
(so-called for the EU passport lane at the airport, their joke) to say
You must come to this show. You mud. Bodies of earth, of fire,
of celluloid. Leaf drawing on amate bark paper, invocation
of Itiba Cahubaba calling back to Cuba from her residency in Italy. That crime
scene photograph. Moustaches of her hair. Body. Trace. Images hover in the hot air
above the dirty river. Tomorrow it may stop at Gravesend, M says,
where Pocahontas' body is buried. There to here. River. Will it need
a blue passport to re-enter the country from *la Manche*? Tilting
at windmills, T says, as they cross to the wild side, haunt of bears,
sex workers and Shagsberd, that queer. Outside the walls, plaguelands
turned tourist theme park. M tells how she attempted to sell her
Fimo reproductions of Louise Bourgeois' Turbine Hall staircases
to the Tate shop, the year it opened. What's Fimo asks T. A few miles
east, in her new studio (priced out of the old East End she has come
here to New Cross, in a ramshackle market near King of Hearts where
she got her merman tattoo), she shows them. Fimo. Play-doh. For when
her hands & heart shake too much to work porcelain. *Thinskinned*
what the gallery suggested she call the installation. *Thinksinned* she kept
typing it in emails she never sent. Flush of rage throbs against her
still. No she does not sell seashells. Hulk smash. By their potsherds
ye shall know them. I should have called it *Midden* she says to T. No
they say *Ostrakoi*. What's that? Shells, they say, fragments of shells
used as voting tokens in Athens, to decide whether someone should be
exiled. Hence: ostracism. They hand her a cup of tea – camomile
and limeflower, tisane, with honey from their neighbour's urban hives;
T *secretes*, still, after a decade she cannot work out where these endless
gifts come from, the sweetness appearing out of thin air, prestidigitated
though they are pocketless and carry only a small, battered (no, *distrait*
and not artfully but lifefully) leather backpack slung by a cord – and
demonstrate on some of her sherds, voting the gallery owner out
of the Big Brother house aka the London artworld. But after shells,
or when they ran out of oysters, I don't know, they used potsherds
or *psephos*, pebbles hence psephology, the study of voting. Not of
pseuds says Medusa, but she is smiling. *Ostrakoi*. It crunches in her teeth
(look: cookies!, ginger snaps. Not biscuits which are something
else, when they are at home; soft and warm). Can you cast an oyster? Have you ever, asks T.

What? And they – suddenly shy – gesture. Like Cynthia Plaster-Caster. Who?
Oh. No. But. She has the plaster, the muslin, the vaseline/s. They play
on Spotify (*son of a gun*) as they set aside their cocks to cast
(as if, as they have done) their votes, immortalised in
plaster held in tender hands. To remain
unpainted.

WHAT THE WASTE LAND SAID

Breeding deadland, that's what you call it: the great mystic swamp
of my vagina burnishing gold into barnacle, mineral.
Grrrlchemy: we take what you prize &
trash it. Rub our slime on it, glide on our self-extrusion and call it
good. Your precious metals, your spell books, your scientific
method have annihilated us too long. But at point zero
there is quantum energy, this fission. Shit atom/gold
atom/lack atom. The ions dance & we dance
with them, transforming. All the long spring, transforming
your gated badlands, sewage banks. Spew and sump, slurry of liquidity.

Yumyum honey stomach. Who needs digestion when there's architecture
to be done. What we carry we carry for the generations (we forget). What
we pass from mouth to mouth. What other work is there. Lining up at the
flowerbed, waiting for the honeysuckle to truck with us. You, you and you:
hop on. Zero hours buzz. Among us, premenstrual, all that honeyblood
(say: gubbins, bucket, rusted empire, emergence: zygotic). And all that
bleedout earns no stripes for bumbled stoners. Where the bee's fucked.
Every flower a cancer stick, ashpollen an addiction. Consume until honey
stomach aches. Collapses in on. Now. Time to sweat the sweet stuff.

All. Gone. We: nettles. We: mosquitoes. We: reedbeds. We: salt
eating. We: waste and waste and waste of sungold
turned (only) into green and flight. We rainthroat. We pucker-in-the-mud.
We shale and marsh and sea cabbage in the shadowing
of the power, station. We refresh, birdsnest, resist. Unsettle: take your eucalyptus
argument and tell it to the marsh. Your farms, your fence, your moneyboxes,
your fracking cocks melt. Thaw, resolve in us. Drain/deny. We (are lilacs) rise.

ON HOUSING   ROUNDTABLE

Where do you live? Over a decades-long housing crisis in the UK, the answer to that question has become a complicated one. Our responsibilities and abilities as individuals to put down roots and participate in communities, to invest in the houses we live in and the areas that surround them, have been compromised by years of an unregulated private rental market, unaffordable home ownership and, above all, underinvestment by central government and local councils in the building of new social housing.

Today, one person in every two hundred in England and Wales is homeless. In the first four months of 2018, over 100,000 children in England were living in temporary accommodation, a figure that was up nearly 80 per cent since 2011. In his book about social housing in Britain, *Municipal Dreams*, John Boughton notes that in 1979, one in three of the population lived in council housing. Today, there are more people living in private rental accommodation than in social housing. A report produced by a cross-party commission in the wake of the Grenfell Tower fire called for three million social homes to be built by 2040. And yet in cities up and down the country, but most acutely in London, luxury apartments go up at an alarming speed. The optics can be confusing, as can the economics. Who are these homes for? Who can afford to live there?

This is the context in which our roundtable on housing took place. Our conversation focused on social housing, which once provided genuinely affordable accommodation for the many. The participants traced a history from the beginning of social housing to the effects of Right to Buy to the Grenfell Tower fire in 2017. They discussed the psychological effects of bad housing, the vilification of estates as well as the joyful aspects of growing up in them, the failure of the private market, and how the negative consequences of gentrification might be lessened. As this roundtable shows, a conversation about housing is always a conversation about public space and community, as well as about safety and freedom.

ŽELJKA MAROŠEVIĆ   Where do you all live and where did you grow up?

BRIDGET MINAMORE   I live in Peckham. I live a solid half a mile away from where I was born and half a mile slightly to the left of where I grew up. I was born on Denmark Hill and I grew up in a big estate on Dog Kennel Hill which straddles the border between East Dulwich, Peckham and Camberwell, three very different parts of south London with very different social histories. When I left home and went to university I moved around London but came back to the south-east a few years ago and back to Peckham a year and a half ago.

JOHN BOUGHTON   I was brought up in a seaside resort, Sheringham, on the north Norfolk coast. I lived there until I was eighteen, a nice idyllic childhood, I guess. My parents had bought their home – or rather were paying for it on a mortgage – but, of course, I had friends and close relatives living in council housing so that was part of my world too, as it was for most people. After university in Manchester, I've lived in various places across the country, always in private rental, even when working full-time as a teacher. I was in my thirties when I bought my first home, and I could only do that when my parents died and I could put my share of the money from the house sale towards a deposit. Incidentally, the house I bought in Winchester in 1992 for £57,000 was on sale last year for £415,000. I couldn't afford it currently. I've lived in Spitalfields in London for about ten years now – in the self-proclaimed buzzy gentrifying hipster area, though I'm not sure I particularly belong to that milieu myself. We own the flat – not ex-council – but we've got a nice 1930s council block just behind. Not surprising given that at peak over 80 per cent of the people in Tower Hamlets lived in council homes. That's one reason for my interest in social housing – I'm a social historian and it's been such a huge but neglected part of people's lived experience. Apart from that, the politics has always been important to me – I was active in Labour politics for a long period and was a councillor for a while, representing a large council estate. So it's been a subject close to my heart for a long time and one that seems as important now as ever.

SERAPHIMA KENNEDY   I was born in my mum's council flat in west London, in Earl's Court, which is a weird place to live because it's one of those transient areas between two other areas which are very well off. Earl's Court in the 80s was a hub for Australian backpackers and people who were generally running away from something. I lived there until I was eighteen, and my mum still lives there now. In the last couple of years council housing in that borough has taken on extra weight and significance because my mum's flat is owned and managed by the Royal Borough of Kensington and Chelsea, which is the same local authority that had responsibility for Grenfell Tower.

Now, I live in Kentish Town. I've lived there for about ten years. I prefer Kentish Town to west London because I find the inequality in west London so stark. But that comes with a slight sense of loss, because I've known since I was a child that I would never be able to live anywhere near my mum. She's lived in the same flat since 1976, which is around the same time that Grenfell and lots of other social blocks in that area were constructed. All across England, actually.

MAROŠEVIĆ   I want to focus on social housing for a while because when we're talking about housing, what we're talking about is housing for everyone. But when we talk about social housing now, what do we mean? Who uses that housing, who is it for?

KENNEDY   When I was growing up in the 80s, social housing was for lots of different types of people. And I'd say that even twelve years ago, when I started working in housing – I worked in housing before moving into the arts – housing communities were often very mixed. What I have seen over the past three decades is that it's become much more polarised. And that, generally, the only people who can acquire a social housing tenancy tend to be the most vulnerable in society, and the people with the fewest options about how and where to live. I don't know if that experience or observation matches up with all of yours?

MINAMORE   I grew up later, in the 90s, in a council flat which had an extra bedroom and it was given to my parents because no one wanted to live on our estate. For me, in the 90s, and in the schools I went to, council housing was for poorer kids. I was acutely aware of the fact that I was – maybe not working class, I don't think I really had any of that language – but I was definitely not rich. Those were the definitions we had: rich and not rich. And I was not rich, because we lived in a flat rather than a house. It's only now that I realise everyone who lived in a flat was in council housing. I remember over the 90s and the early 2000s that separation growing bigger between rich and not rich. But now, and I think it's very different outside of London, but in London, the vast majority of people I know who live in council houses are living in Right to Buy ex-council flats. And I'm someone who lives in one as well now, because that's the only place that I can afford.

In London, if you're between, let's say, 25 and 35 and you're renting a houseshare, you're either in a large Victorian house that has been cut up or you're in an ex-council block with a private landlord – I should be specific about that. I now have my parents' friends living in council accommodation side by side with my friends and peers. It's really bizarre and I think it's a miserable consequence of Right to Buy.

COUNCIL ESTATES; RIGHT TO BUY; SHAME

MAROŠEVIĆ   Can you unpick what's strange about it?
MINAMORE   I really find it hard to articulate how I felt... I guess it was shame, when I realised we didn't have any money in our family. I'm lucky in the fact that my parents lived together and both worked, and I'm an only child. And yet we still had next to no money. I sometimes think about how, you know, I don't think my parents collectively ever earned more than £30,000, like ever, at any point. So now whenever I hear people talk about middle-class salaries, I have a moment where I go, 'Oh God', because to me, those amounts are huge. That amount of money was what my parents said they wanted to earn, and they didn't get anywhere close to it. To be really aware of the fact that our council flat was a council flat and our housing was a representation of, not poverty, but being, I guess, working class, to now voluntarily live in the council space, in the working class space – I'm using these inverted comma fingers – is bizarre.

My friends who didn't grow up in council houses consider what they pay to be cheap. For me, to pay that much to live in a council flat is ridiculous. I have a landlord who is relatively alright and doesn't charge us a massive amount, but my rent is still twice what my parents paid for their three bedroom flat. My parents balk at what I pay. They are like, 'How is this possible?' Yet I pay a third less than all of my friends because I still have enough connections in the area to find people who aren't going to hike up the rents. You get people paying £700, £800 to live in a houseshare in Peckham, which to me is absolutely diabolical.

No one wanted to live on the estate I grew up on for a really long time. And now half of it is bought up by people who want to send their kids to the private schools in Dulwich. To see that happen at a rapid pace, within my living memory from the beginning of secondary school to adulthood, is almost unbelievable. It's possible to recognise that change regardless of all the facts and the figures. I can see for myself the changing demographics of this area.

My mum worked as a short-term foster carer and I remember when one of her friends said, 'If you're renting, you need to be careful because they'll push you out. You need to buy your flat.' My parents didn't want to buy their flat. In Ghana, where they're from, renting long-term is not a strange thing. So they were very happy to rent forever, when they were together anyway. But my parents took the advice and used Right to Buy and a year or two later the Bedroom Tax came in, which would have kicked them out immediately. I really struggle with that as well because Right to Buy shouldn't be for them. They eventually want to retire to Ghana, but they knew they'd be forced out of their home. In an ideal world the council would come and take their flat and swap it with them, right? Or, when they were splitting up, they could have each got a small one-bedroom flat. And suddenly a big beautiful three-bedroom would be let out for a family. Because of the precariousness of renting and the way councils work now, they knew that unless they bought it, they wouldn't have any claim on it. To me that's the saddest outcome of all. They aren't people who wanted to own their property, they were very happy as long as they had a bit of security and safety. And what's happened is that now that property is off the market to council tenants forever. That's really sad. I loved that home. It's 1930s, beautiful brick, built to last, and now it's gone.

OVERCROWDING; MENTAL PRESSURE; THE BEDROOM TAX

KENNEDY   I'd echo what you were saying, Bridget, about the shame and stigma that can come with growing up in social housing, but often this is about conditions affecting all types of tenure. One of the brilliant things about London, historically, is the diversity of communities in terms of income and background. But there's the external stigma that's applied to living in social housing, and then also a kind of internal stigma that comes with, for example, living in poor quality accommodation, living in homes where mould and damp are almost designed into the building because of the poor quality of the construction materials or successive pieces of legislation which don't force local authorities or private landlords to actually look after homes properly. And there are also issues to do with overcrowding.

I'd say overcrowding was for me the most significant one. When you grow up in an overcrowded home, which is also a council home, and your parents just don't have the means to move you on, the impact is huge.

MAROŠEVIĆ   Because they physically did not have space for themselves?

KENNEDY   Yeah, absolutely. The impact of not being able to do homework; the impact of having asthma and being taken to the doctor and overhearing conversations where the doctor is explaining that it's caused by the mould in your bedroom or bathroom. These are conditions that people are living in all across the country every single day. And yet we don't hear about the impact of overcrowding.

One of the things I think we forget about is that the right to adequate housing is actually an economic, social and cultural right enshrined in various instruments of international law. States have a responsibility to provide adequate housing, 'a secure place to live for human dignity, physical and mental health and overall quality of life'. Bridget mentioned the Bedroom Tax. When that was introduced in 2014 a UN Special Rapporteur on adequate housing, Raquel Rolnik, came over – the UN has sent two to the UK in the past few years – and she said that housing isn't just about bricks and mortar, it's about human dignity and wellbeing. That seems to have been lost from the discussion around what housing is for and who it's for. By that I don't just mean social housing, actually. There are issues around the private provision of housing as well, and the way that people are going to bed at the moment in some tower blocks in fear of their lives because of the cladding that's still on their buildings. It's been two years since Grenfell, and still the government hasn't taken adequate steps to ensure safety.

MAROŠEVIĆ   In John's book *Municipal Dreams*, he discusses the public vs private dichotomy. In the past few decades we've seen a repeated insistence from successive governments that it doesn't matter what happens to social housing because the private market will take over; the private market will provide. Whereas actually people have the same issues with mould and overcrowding in private rentals and landlords don't have any reason to do anything about it because they know how competitive the market is and how easily tenants can be replaced.

MINAMORE   What we're getting now is that mentality in social housing.

KENNEDY   Absolutely.

MINAMORE   The vast majority of people I know, especially in cities, live badly by default. I said my landlord was great but that's only because she leaves us alone. That shouldn't be the bar.

KENNEDY   It's not just privatisation either, because over the past few decades power has been firmly put into the hands of local authorities and taken away from tenants.

'A HOUSING REVOLUTION'

BOUGHTON   I guess what you've been talking about in different ways is a housing revolution. And not a good one. Since 1979, essentially, when Margaret Thatcher came to power, we've lost 2.5 million social homes through Right to Buy. We have 1.5 million fewer council houses now than we had forty years ago. And 40 per cent of those properties that were sold through Right to Buy are now in the private rental sector. So it's created a huge pressure on social housing, leading to the issues you're describing. Of course, at the same time the private rental sector has expanded enormously. Back in 1979, the private rental sector was pretty minimal, whereas now there are more people living in private rental housing than in social housing.

MINAMORE   It is a revolution.

BOUGHTON   It's put enormous pressure on the social housing that remains. As you say, Bridget, the private rental sector is pretty unregulated. Despite all the laws and regulations that ostensibly cover 'fitness for purpose', most of them are never enforced.

It's interesting talking about the stigma that's been attached to social housing because if you look at the longer story, that wasn't the case. It was always the case, I think into the 60s, that council housing was pretty much the pick of the crop. It was what people aspired to. And you hear so many stories from over the last century of people moving into their first council homes from slum conditions. Even the council flats we can see through the window here in Deptford – the typical, London five-storey walk-up balcony-access blocks – were described as Buckingham Palace or Shangri La by the people moving into them.

I think what changed over the longer term, perhaps beginning from the 1960s, was the rise of owner-occupation, which did spread to the working classes. So at that point council housing moved from being at the top of the tree to slightly inferior accommodation, at least psychologically. In the 1970s, after the mass public housing drive of the previous decade, some of the conditions that you were describing, Seraphima, in terms of poor quality construction and the problems that causes, were very well publicised, and powerfully felt if you were living in those homes, and that created a negative narrative of council housing. But everything for me relates back to Right to Buy and the virtual halt on building council housing from the 1980s onwards. The jargon is 'residualisation'. You effectively have social housing becoming residualised, i.e. increasingly confined to the poorest, the most vulnerable.

FEAR

MAROŠEVIĆ   Why do you think the British are so obsessed with owning property? In continental Europe most people rent for their whole lives. Where did the idea come from that we need to possess the place we live in?
MINAMORE   In terms of my parents' attitude, I can't speak for all of West Africa and say that people don't care about property, but it's just very different. If you flatten a patch of land in London and build a house you're a multi-millionaire, right? Whereas in Ghana it's much more common to buy land and build your own home. But in the cities there everyone is renting and the tenancies are long-term because security is valued. In parts of Europe where people rent for their whole lives, it's to do with security and the fact that you have more rights as a tenant. People place value on the fact that tenants want to feel at home, that a house is not just a space to store your things and somewhere to sleep. It's an emotional, almost spiritual place. It should be a space where we all feel safe, particularly children or people who are vulnerable in other ways.

When you look at things in this country like the skyrocketing rates of child poverty, or people with disabilities living in poverty, a lot of that comes hand in hand with the fact that housing is getting worse. You have more children growing up in substandard housing and disabled people battling bureaucracies to get money for housing, and that affects the way you feel about your home.

When I was a kid, we tried to get rehoused because of a really horrible incident that happened in our house. And it was hell, it was absolute hell. I loved my home and my community. I knew everyone on the estate. It was a massive estate and yeah, there were various illegal things going on, but broadly, it was very safe. I couldn't go back to the house for a year because I was so terrified of what had happened, which was separate to how I felt about the estate. Being on the waiting list for a new house was the worst thing about it. To this day, almost twenty years later, the trauma around that time is one of the worst things that has ever happened to me.

We moved into horrible temporary accommodation that was cockroach- and rat-infested, which is what a lot of temporary accommodation is like. When I think of the residents of Grenfell who are still in temporary accommodation two years later it makes me want to cry. I remember so acutely the feeling of not being able to stay in that accommodation because it was that bad. I stayed with an aunt in her box-room for a year. We wrote letters to MPs, we did everything you're supposed to do, and eventually we got to the point where we realised we'd just have to move back to our flat because we weren't going to get rehoused. They were offering us tiny, tiny places instead and physically the three of us could not move into spaces that small – it would not have been suitable for a pre-teen girl and her parents.

This isn't a unique story by any means. And so when I think of the mental toll of dealing with the current housing system as it is, it's diabolical. I can't think how badly the next generation of children are going to be affected. Even if overnight these housing issues were solved, we'd still be feeling the effects of this crisis for decades, through the people that lived through it.

TEMPORARY ACCOMMODATION;
COMMUNITY; THE QUEEN MUM

KENNEDY   We seem to have forgotten the reasons why social housing exists in the first place.

The mental toll you've been describing, Bridget, is something I've observed time and time again. When I used to be a housing officer and I'd sign someone up for their tenancy, they'd tell me that they'd been in temporary accommodation for ten years. When you have someone coming through the housing system today they have had to fight so hard to get there before they've even been given a home. And they've maybe lived in ten, twelve, twenty different places; their kids have gone to six or seven different schools. I've heard women who have been survivors of domestic violence refusing to go into temporary accommodation, even though the police have been telling them they're at risk. They didn't want to go into the temporary accommodation system because they had just finally come out of it.

Once you're in temporary accommodation you get stuck in it. It just takes so long. You constantly have to provide piece after piece of information. If anyone in your family has special needs you have to fight for psychological assessments and medical assessments. It's absolutely degrading, and verges on the inhumane more often than not, I would say. It's very far removed from the idea of fair housing for all, which was behind the initial house building programs, which were also a response to the proliferation of slum dwellings.

John, it was really good that you raised the positive aspects of living in social housing. There's an estate near Grenfell called the Henry Dickens estate. When I worked around there I remember one of the residents told me that the Queen Mum came and visited the construction site when it was being built. I don't know if it was actually the Queen Mum, but that highlighted to me how proud she was of where she lived, and how for her family this was seen as something that was really desirable. It's important to recognise that social housing is often a really positive thing for the people who live in it, and it can provide safety and security for all citizens who live in it.

MINAMORE   And community as well.

KENNEDY   Absolutely.

MINAMORE   I absolutely loved my estate for so much of my childhood. I would observe the kids I went to school with who lived in these big semi-detached houses, and they couldn't know fifty people on their road, because that was their whole road. Whereas it was very easy for me. We lived in the middle of the estate so if I walked from the top to the bottom I would see so many people

I knew and people would throw things over the balconies to give to my parents. Now when you're separated by people who are private tenants for a short period of time, it does break up the feeling of community. And it's a real shame because I think that's something that social housing in this country has done really well for a long time. It's sad that we're actively destroying it.

KENNEDY   There are very specific policies that have been designed to to push social housing tenants out of London. Not least the Localism Act of 2011 which enabled councils to meet their duty of care by offering private rented accommodation that didn't have to be in-borough. That's a very specific and deliberate piece of legislation. Your question was about ownership and this is an example of how the rights of social tenants have been taken away and given to private landlords.

BOUGHTON   The irony, of course, is that home ownership has declined in Britain in recent years. It peaked at around 71 per cent in 2003 and is now at around 63 per cent, which is below the western European average.

MAROŠEVIĆ   So who owns all the properties?

BOUGHTON   It's Right to Buy and Buy to Let.

KENNEDY   And private landlords. There was a study in the *Guardian* recently which showed that there are a huge number of private landlords in London alone who own about five Right to Buy properties each, many of which are leased back to local authorities in order to provide temporary accommodation for those who they have accepted onto the waiting list.

'WE HAVE TO KNOW THE VALUE OF SOMETHING RATHER THAN THE COST.'

BOUGHTON   We live in an Alice in Wonderland situation. Only a couple of weeks ago, the *Guardian* was reporting that councils are actually paying private landlords a bribe – not rent or anything like that – but an actual bribe to incentivise them to accept homeless households.

To go back to the question about ownership, I think there was a broad consensus after 1945 that the state had a duty towards its citizenry. Obviously that applied to health, and resulted in the NHS, but it certainly applied to housing too. There was an expectation that the state had a basic duty to provide decent, affordable housing to all of the population. But I think some of the shine and sheen had fallen from that by the 1970s. When Thatcher came into power in '79 there was a real sense of the ideology shifting. She articulated the new right-wing ideology of the time, which was private good, public bad. In her terms, that was a property-owning democracy. There's a certain idealism around that too, from that political perspective. But of course in practice it's been disastrous.

What you see really from the economic crisis of the mid-70s onwards, is this sense of public spending as being anathema. And we've lost – this might be changing now, I hope it is – that sense of investment. Investment in people, investment in communities. If you invest in housing, if you spend money building social housing, that's the finest investment you can make in any individual, any child. That's what Bridget was describing. We really need to retrieve that sense. We have to know what the value of something is rather than the cost. KENNEDY   That's what the Shelter commission that was set up post-Grenfell calls for actually: a massive investment in social housing over a prolonged period of time.

I think there's a positive aspect to Right to Buy, which it might be useful to acknowledge, and that's the impact for individual families. Perhaps that's a political impact, actually, because maybe you're more likely to be grateful to those in power if you're able to buy and sell your home. For those families who benefit from it I think they would probably see Right to Buy as a good thing. My sister and her partner are proper grafters and they worked their way into home ownership through a council tenancy. On the other hand, it's absolutely decimated the ability of the state to provide homes for people, for normal people. MINAMORE   It can be positive on an individual level. It's funny, when you were talking about overcrowding Seraphima, I always forget to point out the fact that our house was always hugely full because we had an extra box-room. There were only three of us but in immigrant working class communities, you don't just live alone. You always have various cousins or quote-unquote cousins, aunties and uncles staying with you, often without Right to Work papers, often in this country illegally, although I don't like using that term for people. Despite all that, I really did enjoy living in that home for a long time.

I understand the arguments for Right to Buy on an individual level. But again, I'd go back to the question of whether there's a need to have homeownership beyond just making money? Maybe that's the only reason. But I feel like, if the benefit of owning a home is that no one can force you out of it, if we had that security within social housing, how many people would really need to own their homes?

I think we just have a really odd approach to housing in this country. In Ghana, you don't have extra rooms in your house. You have rooms for family, but you know who you're building that bedroom for before you build your home. At my aunt's house, I have a bedroom because I go there every year and when I'm not there, a relative stays in it. I don't understand this idea of having extra empty space. Why wouldn't you just have a bigger living space so you could invite more people in?

LUXURY FLATS

MINAMORE   There's an old estate in Camberwell that is absolutely stunning, right next to the Green. I remember going in once – it was for sale and I wanted to have a poke around. It had high windows and high ceilings and I thought, 'How could this be a council or housing association property?' And then I thought no, it was built for people to enjoy living here. And that doesn't often happen anymore.

A friend of mine was talking about the luxury flats being built on Queens Road Peckham. I can see them from my window. I have a view of Canary Wharf from my window which will soon be gone because they're building these flats. My friend asked me, are they private or public? I said there are claims that a certain percentage will be public but I'm not optimistic. And my friend said, 'Isn't that bleak? That when you say luxury flats, we assume it can't be for the public, it can't be for the working classes.' And I just thought, 'Oh my God, yeah.' When I say 'luxury flats' I mean they're being built too nicely so of course they can't be for the public. The problem is so deep-rooted. The approach we have to housing, the approach we have to space, is all wrong. We need to be able to say, no, we don't just need houses, we need lots of space, especially in a city that's so crowded and so busy and so difficult. Space should be important; bedrooms should be twice as big. MAROŠEVIĆ   I was born in Bosnia but grew up in Greater Manchester, in Stockport. My family moved through a series of council houses and then my parents bought a house, which is an ex-council house, when I was eleven. I remember when my family moved from a privately rented house we'd been paying for with housing benefit onto a purpose-built estate, the windows were so much smaller. You immediately noticed the windows were half the size. It was like, 'Why would you assume we would want less light?'

KENNEDY   A lot of the older tower blocks were built to the Parker Morris standards. But they aren't used now. Now it's these kind of rabbit hutch developments that we see going up all over the place. Giorgio Agamben has this concept of 'bare life'. Instead of thinking about what communities and individuals need to flourish, it's like, what can we get away with?

MAROŠEVIĆ   What's the bare minimum?

MINAMORE   It's like the minimum wage compared to the living wage.

KENNEDY   Yeah, how many can we cram in here? And that's a really infectious thing. Last year another UN Special Rapporteur for housing, Leilani Farha, came to the UK. She visited the Latimer community in west London. She talked about the financialisation of housing, her concern that residents hadn't been seen as human beings, and the constant emphasis on the amount of money that can be brought in from housing. So even when you look at regeneration or redevelopment of existing areas of social housing, social landlords are considering how many other units they can squeeze in – not just for social rent but for affordable rent, which can be up to 80 per cent of market rent. Up to 80 per cent of market rent in Westminster or Kensington is obviously unaffordable for the majority of people. It's this idea of the amount of money that can be extracted from the units, rather than who the units are for. Even the word 'unit' – they're homes, aren't they?

BOUGHTON   The quality of homes reflects what we were discussing earlier, which is the decline in public investment. Since the 1980s local authorities have been forced into public-private partnerships. In the good old days it was very easy for local authorities to borrow money. They could borrow money directly from the government at very low interest rates from the Public Works Loans Board, which was a very cost-effective way of delivering investment capital to local authorities. That was ended in the 1980s.

MAROŠEVIĆ   Did that change come from government?

BOUGHTON   That came from government diktat as part of the Thatcherite drive towards privatisation. I would compliment local authorities in the sense that many of them, basically all of them, want to build homes. But in order to do so they've been forced into these public-private partnerships and have been forced to make those calculations that Seraphima was describing.

Invariably, even in the new builds, most of those homes will be either for sale or for private rent at so-called affordable rents. If you're lucky there will be some social housing. And this all reflects the crazy economics that housing has been forced into since the 1980s.

'THE PEOPLE AT THE BEGINNING
OF THE CHANGE ARE NEVER AT THE
END OF THE CHANGE.'

KENNEDY   Those affordable-housing homes are great for young professionals, they're great if you're mobile, if you have means. They're not if you're someone who's just born in the area and isn't necessarily mobile in that way, and doesn't have the same access to capital. For them – us! – it's often impossible to stay there and grow with the economy. It comes down to: what do you want from a community?

MINAMORE   A lot of people do want community, I think. But even if you are, let's say, a young professional or a student, and you're paying all this money to live in a new flat, you might not go and embrace the community because the gentrification conversation is often so fraught. You can see that things are changing and you can tell that you're not part of the original community. And so a lot of the time, you don't try to be part of it in a way that's constructive. The biggest reason I moved back to south London from east London was because I moved to Hackney Wick the year of the Olympics and it was bizarre to be this interloper where you know that things are changing and that people aren't happy. You're surrounded by people who are being pushed out of their homes while you're moving there. It just felt too strange and uncomfortable to me, so now I've moved back to south London where I'm on the other end and I'm just cross about everything all of the time.

You're endlessly irritated by what's happening to your home – that cafe is new and the market stalls can't afford their rent and the railway arches are going to go. I do understand that change must happen. But it's very clear that the change is not for us. The people at the beginning of the change are never at the end of the change. There are ways for this change to be wider and for everyone.

MAROŠEVIĆ   How could the effects of those changes be softened? How could they be more thoughtful?

MINAMORE   Give power back to the community. In Peckham, for example, there's this new development called Peckham Palms. In the way that anything new gets an eyeroll, I remember seeing it and thinking, what's this? Then I found out that one of the people running it was heavily involved in the 'Reclaim Brixton' project, which is an anti-gentrification project just down the road. She told me people wanted to build a unit in a big empty space behind the car park. And she told them, 'Well, if I come in, people will actually listen and care.' So they got her on board, gave her a paid job, and they've given the unit to some of the hairdressers on Rye Lane who have been shoved out because of the new National Rail developments. They've had to do works on the railway for a while and they've used it as an excuse to get rid of all the businesses in the arches.

MAROŠEVIĆ   Which is exactly what they did in Brixton.

MINAMORE   Exactly, but in Brixton they didn't put those businesses anywhere new. In this case, almost all of the people working in those hairdressers are immigrant, African, Caribbean working-class women. The hairdressers are places where you can keep your kids with you while you work and it's quite safe. These women would have been kicked out with nowhere to go. At the same time, that development is having yoga classes in the mornings and music gigs. But I was like, Well, here, look at it. You have this new project but you also have people from the community being able to continue their livelihoods, black people from the community running the yoga classes and hosting events. It's very new but I'm optimistic about it. This is what I want to happen. We can do things to give power and money back to communities and help that cycle be a little less rough, a little less aggressive, and a little less hostile to the people who've always been there. But only a small percentage of those women made it into that unit. I wonder what's happened to the rest of the hairdressers. They're probably working out of houses again, which is, I guess, technically illegal so they're at risk of prosecution. I worry about them.

GENTRIFICATION; THE LONDON RIOTS

MINAMORE   We don't talk much about the London Riots any more but that's a big part of this city's history. It's no surprise to me that the areas where things were most fraught were areas where people were battling their own gentrification struggles – places like Peckham, Brixton or Croydon. Places where you were suddenly getting this clash of people.

MAROŠEVIĆ   Do you think the riots were a reaction to gentrification?

MINAMORE   I think we live in a time where space is moneyed. The estates we used to hang out on, or the balconies, half of them have been bought by people who would tell you to get off. There are ten houses on each balcony and five of them are now occupied by young professionals who, fairly I guess, don't want large groups of young black teenagers on their balconies. The youth club doesn't exist anymore. Neither does the Connexions Centre. Where are you going to go? What are you going to do? And then there's the fear of Stop and Search. It builds and builds. I work with a lot of young people from the inner city and they don't have the spaces to hang out in that I had. Literally every space where I used to hang out in south-east London does not exist anymore. What else are they supposed to do? The kids have to go out and embrace that tension. And that's why things kick off.

'IF YOU CAN'T SEE A FUTURE FOR YOURSELF, THEN YOUR FUTURE DOESN'T EXIST.'

KENNEDY   I wrote a piece on knife crime last year because I walked home past the scene of two murders in one night. And what Bridget is saying came up again and again – the mental pressure, overcrowding, the lack of opportunity to move. Also, what it means for young people watching their parents work ridiculously hard and still not being able to see themselves having a future in their community because 'affordable housing' isn't affordable and you can't get on the social housing register. So all of that does contribute, I think, to a really toxic combination of pressures on young people, boys and girls. Those young people are much more vulnerable to being exploited by older gang members, and everything that can come from that. If you can't see a future for yourself, then your future doesn't exist. So what is the point of going to school, getting your qualifications and working hard? It didn't help your parents; how's it going to help you?

MAROŠEVIĆ   I want to circle back to the question of architecture and how houses are designed to suit people's lives. It's been clear as we've been talking that it's not just houses that are important but the spaces and facilities around them. John, are there good examples of estates where architects thought holistically about people's lives?

BOUGHTON   I think it's important to emphasise that public housing originally was built to high standards. Seraphima mentioned the Parker Morris standards, which were introduced in 1961, and they applied to public housing but not to private. In fact, the housing minister of the day said they should set an example for the private sector to follow; it was something to emulate. Even today private housing at the cheaper end of the market tends to be rabbit-hutch housing and very poorly constructed. It's not a model by any means.

Without being starry-eyed, council housing was pretty well-built, decent, affordable, certainly. At best there was an ambition to provide not only a good home but a decent space, including play areas and green areas. In the post-war period, the ideal was to create community, and to provide community centres, youth centres and drop-in centres for old people. There was an ideal to create and foster community. Not always fulfilled, but that was the aspiration. There are many good examples of that across London. Camden's built some wonderful estates. I really like the Churchill Gardens Estate in Westminster, actually built by a Conservative council but high quality and still very much loved and valued by the people who live in it – now a very mixed community and lots of it Right to Buy. That estate seems to have functioned very well to the present, and more recently they put in a community garden.

Ironically, the right-wing ideal currently is to create streets and to follow the middle-class model of traditional terraced or semi-detached houses. But actually if you look at earlier council estates, what you see are shared spaces that were well used and valued by the people who lived there. So I think actually you can look to that model as being a preferable one to the traditional suburbs.

HUMAN RIGHTS; REVOLVING DOORS

KENNEDY   You asked earlier about what needs to change. I think it's really important to think about the attitudinal change that needs to take place. When you view housing as a source of income, either for a private landlord or local authority, you lose sight of the fact that it's human beings who live there. It's really obvious but it doesn't seem to feature much in the language around housing or regeneration.

It's something that was picked up by Leilani Farha, the UN Special Rapporteur for housing, when she visited last year. Human beings have rights. This sounds really basic. We are holders of rights; we are holders of the right to adequate housing. States have a positive duty to uphold those rights. It might seem weird to bring the language of human rights into a conversation about social housing but I think that is so important. Actually, if we understand ourselves to be the holders of rights that the state has an obligation to protect, rather than to diminish, surely that would lead to the attitudinal shift that is needed in central policy and in housing offices. It's definitely not something that's considered on the front line by those who are administering housing on behalf of the state and who often bring their own prejudices and discriminatory behaviours to the job.

On a more practical level, it's about meaningful engagement. If people aren't meaningfully engaged when it comes to talking about redevelopment or regeneration, they don't have a voice. And if they don't have a voice, they're not being given basic rights and dignities. This suits some politicians, there's a revolving door between local councillors, local authorities and private developers. We know that local councillors will often work in planning committees and then go off and consult privately with local authorities about how to get around planning legislation and how to bypass the laws that are supposed to protect us. This information is out there but it gets kind of lost in the mix. We should all be outraged.

GRENFELL

MAROŠEVIĆ   John, in your book you write: 'Here is the value, the absolute necessity, of the health and safety measures so widely derided in recent years. And if "austerity" can sometimes seem a piece of empty political rhetoric, this is its reality. For almost four decades, we have been taught the neoliberal mantra, "private good, public bad" and encouraged to see public spending as an evil; ruthless economising as a virtue. We have come to know the price of everything and the value of nothing and have ended with the funeral pyre of Grenfell Tower.'

KENNEDY   It is very hard to talk about even two years on. It didn't happen to me, but it's hard to talk about for all of us, and and should continue to be, because there is a danger of Grenfell itself becoming empty political rhetoric. There's a danger of austerity and Grenfell in the same sentence being a kind of easy equivocation. That isn't the right word, it's more complicated than that. But ultimately, what Grenfell teaches us is that the failure of public policy in relation to housing is death. Grenfell shows why it matters.

I find it hard to talk about because it's so frustrating. We saw the same mistakes before Grenfell at Ronan Point and Lakanal House in Camberwell. The inquest reported on Lakanal in 2012. We have all this knowledge and information on how policies should change to protect the lives of citizens, and yet it's not being implemented. And it's not being implemented in the context of a really hostile environment. It's hard not to feel very disheartened by that. This is why there needs to be an independent housing regulator. It's something that Grenfell United have called for, and the Shelter commission also recommended it. An independent regulator was set up after the financial crash. Independent regulators have been set up for other industries when lives have not been lost, so there needs to be proper oversight and proper accountability when it comes to policies that affect people in their homes.

FLOWERS; WASHING LINES; FIRE HAZARDS

MINAMORE   I totally agree with that. I think we're in real danger of Grenfell not only becoming empty political rhetoric to be bandied around by politicians, but also being used by local authorities and councils to create hostility in council accommodation.

In my parents' flat, maybe a year after Grenfell, they all got letters through their doors telling them they weren't allowed flowerpots outside their doors and on their balconies, and they weren't allowed to hang washing lines, because they were fire hazards. The council had been trying to get rid of those things for years, and now they were a fire hazard. I remember reading that letter and getting so angry, because the residents' responses were, 'I guess it is a fire hazard so we have to do as we're told.' But it was just another thing for the council to take away from them. They haven't done fire alarm checks on the estate for years. The residents have been asking for checks for years and it's brought up in the residents' meeting every month. The checks still haven't been done, but the washing lines are gone.

One of the older women on my dad's estate was known around the area for having an amazing flower display on her balcony. She had fresh flowers every week, I think someone in her family is a florist. I remember as a kid we'd use her balcony as a meeting point. They were all gone a few days after that letter. I firmly believe that the council want the tenants gone from the estate and private landlords there instead. I tweeted about it and loads of people responded to me with similar stories. I think it's such a depressing and cynical outcome where you can essentially get your tenants to do whatever you want, not quite by making a threat but by referencing Grenfell, which is obviously so fraught in the collective memory.

BOUGHTON   I think one of the big lessons of Grenfell is obviously about power, in terms of who has a voice. And that's been expressed by Grenfell United and it's mentioned by the Shelter commission too. I think hopefully there is a move in that direction. It's ironic, isn't it, because when tenant management organisations were started in the 60s and 70s they were intended to be fairly grassroots and bottom-up organisations. Kensington and Chelsea was a very strange organisation in that sense and by all accounts fairly unresponsive and not a listening authority. So definitely, I think tenants have to be genuinely empowered. Looking at the bigger picture, what we've seen is really the retreat of the state. The state isn't always benign; it can sometimes be oppressive. But essentially the state should have a duty of care towards its citizens. And we've seen a retreat from that duty since the 80s and very clearly and directly in terms of building control, building inspections and deregulation. We've seen building inspectors, who had previously worked for the local authority, who were literally privatised. Building inspection was taken over in many cases by the developers themselves.

KENNEDY   If you're paying someone to say that your building is okay, they're not going to say your building isn't okay.

BOUGHTON   And then more widely, we've seen the weakening of building controls. We had the warning signs from Lakanal House that flammable cladding shouldn't be permitted and in fact regulations had already been changed in Scotland. The unwillingness to act on the evidence and to enforce that duty of care was shocking.

KENNEDY   As well as that, you had things like the red tape initiative, which was launched in 2014. The coalition government had a complete obsession with bureaucracy and red tape. They launched this initiative with the explicit aim of clearing the way for house builders, minimising regulation, interference and scrutiny that they face in order to save them money. This was at the same time as the government was talking about the Big Society and not listening to the concerns raised after the inquest into the deaths at Lakanal House. So you have this really toxic mix of ideologies. But worse than that actually, an active destruction and removal of the safeguards that are supposed to keep homes safe and to keep new buildings safe. They were actually scheduled to meet on the morning of the fire to talk about EU Fire Safety.

I think that lack of care is mirrored in the length of time it's taking for those failures that have been identified so far to be addressed. Just today, actually, *Inside Housing* published a piece about tower blocks, used in social housing and for hotels and student accommodation, which still have the same combination of dangerous ACM cladding. Last year the government introduced some funding for social housing landlords to remove the dangerous cladding, but it hasn't provided any funding for private landlords, so they have to meet the cost themselves, which they've then tried to pass on to leaseholders. So people have mortgaged themselves to the hilt to buy a flat and then they have been told they need to pay £70,000 for the remediation works. Who has £70,000? At the moment in those buildings you have residents taking it in turns to do waking watches because of the speed with which fire travels up those materials. If you watch the videos from the inquiry, it's absolutely remarkable. These people are living in unsafe homes, and they are terrified – it's taking a major toll on the health, life and wellbeing of thousands of people across the country. It's just the most ridiculous, obscene situation. I raised

that simply to say that failure in the duty of care that we saw before Grenfell doesn't seem to have changed and unless it does, there will be another Grenfell in two or five years' time when the threat diminishes from the public mind. We have to make sure that doesn't happen.

ALTERNATIVE HOUSING

MINAMORE   Leading off from that, recently there's been a weird kind of discussion about alternate forms of housing as a solution to the housing crisis, things like housing co-operatives and property guardianships. The reason I could move back to south London was that I lived in a housing co-op, and I have friends in property guardianships, so I have a lot of first-hand experiences with both. Co-ops are fraught with internal politics and often don't live up to the ideals they claim to adhere to. With guardianships, often they are just not fit for purpose, and they're deregulated. You'll have twenty people on the bottom floor of a school with no heating, sharing one portable shower. You have rodents and vermin everywhere, because you're literally almost outside in some parts.

Often when we talk about other forms of housing, co-ops and guardianships are referred to as a solution, simply because they're cheap. They are, but it's not that simple. Actually this is about regulating industries and taking away so much of the money that's involved and changing attitudes towards housing. It shouldn't be the case that alternative forms of housing are slotted in when one form of housing isn't working, especially when that form of housing is state social housing which should be working.

MAROŠEVIĆ   And has worked very well in the past.

KENNEDY   Property guardianship makes me laugh because let's not forget what they're guarding against. They're guarding against squatters. You're taking one group of society who can't afford to rent anywhere because of the housing crisis and positioning them in order to defend property, which is capital, and that shouldn't be standing empty in the first place. It's absolutely shocking.

MINAMORE   Even with housing co-operatives, which are seen as utopias for building communities, people don't talk about how the co-operative model has been bastardised by the crisis. So in Sanford, the co-op I lived in, there were eight to nine people in every house and

our rents technically got cheaper as the years went on because of the co-operative economic model. You have people who've been there for thirty years or for three months; I was there for about three years. There's an idea that the people who live in housing co-operatives are there for the experience of that. But a lot of people there were saving to get on the housing ladder and the low rent was allowing them to save for a deposit. So even the community aspect of the co-op was disappearing, according to a lot
of the people who had been there for years.
BOUGHTON   I think that brings us back to Housing Associations, which were the big hope of the 80s. In some ways, I think they were genuine and positive and fairly unbureaucratic, but then there were these mammoth amalgamations and so many of them have lost any kind of local roots, or local presence, even. Many of them embraced an entrepreneurial vision of seeing themselves primarily as housing developers and began building more houses for sale and for 'affordable' rent. Housing Associations really need to go back to their philanthropic roots and social purpose.
MAROŠEVIĆ   Were Housing Associations originally run by residents?
BOUGHTON   No, but they were certainly community-based. And they were committed to housing local people affordably and decently. That's been lost in many ways. I do think we need to empower local councils to build. We've taken baby steps in that direction in the last couple of years. Even under this ideologically fairly hostile government, councils are being allowed to build again.
MINAMORE   Why is that?
BOUGHTON   There is a recognition, even from the right-wing political perspective, that social housing has to be a part of the mix, that it isn't for everybody, but for any genuinely functional housing market you need social housing.
MAROŠEVIĆ   And who would the current government say that housing is for? Is it again for the most vulnerable or can they see beyond that?
BOUGHTON   While we have such a shortage of housing, we quite rightly have to prioritise those with the greatest needs. Social housing does become, in that sense, a bit of an ambulance service. In order to rectify that problem, I think we need to be building at scale and creating a housing stock which can cater for a wider cross-section of the population, as it did historically.

'THE PEOPLE AREN'T GOING TO GO AWAY.'

KENNEDY   Mixed housing is really beneficial. The discourse around housing often focuses on vulnerability and poverty, but actually mixed housing really works for everyone. Survivors of Grenfell have been outspoken about the fact that they loved their homes; their homes were wonderful. Many of them were working people getting by. That's who housing policy needs to cater for – normal working people who can build families and have a future in communities where they've chosen to build their lives. That might seem like a pipe dream.
MAROŠEVIĆ   John, there's a conversation you quote in your book where Nick Clegg relates a meeting he had when he was in the coalition government. He brought up building social housing and either David Cameron or George Osborne said, 'Why do you keep going on about social housing? Why would we build houses to increase the number of Labour voters?' They could only see it as a political question – why would we build for a voting public that will vote us out?
KENNEDY   Absolutely.
MINAMORE   I mean I can't even. How can housing be a party political point? The people aren't going to go away. You can't get rid of people whether they're in houses or not.
MAROŠEVIĆ   Wherever you put them –
MINAMORE   They exist. We exist.

'THE MARKET REALLY WON'T PROVIDE.'

BOUGHTON   I'm broadly optimistic. My sense is that there are cycles and moments in history. In some respects the post-1945 moment, which lasted probably thirty-odd years, was a social democratic one. There was a consensus across political parties. Of course the largest number of council houses ever built in a single year was built under a Conservative government. They built 229,000 council houses in 1953. That will to house the population well has existed across the political spectrum. Conversely, I think we've lived through forty years of the private good, public bad mantra, this sense that the market will provide. I think now people realise the market really won't provide. It is not designed to cater for needs that cannot be immediately justified by profit. That obviously applies to the NHS, but it clearly also applies to housing. I think the dream of owner-occupation for all has faded, but we do need both a decent social housing sector and a properly regulated and secure private sector. So I think there's a lot that should change, and a lot that might change.

KENNEDY   It's really good that you're optimistic. I just read Carolyn Forché's memoir, *What You Have Heard is True*, which is about El Salvador. Obviously it's a different situation, but there are a couple of lines in the book that I think are really relevant. She says that injustices of a political nature are rarely historical accidents. While I don't think you can attribute motive to state failures of this kind, if you don't put the wheels on your car correctly it's not going to be a surprise if you have an accident on the road, is it? I think there really is an urgent public safety and public health need. She also talks about poverty and corruption that benefit the few, and crimes unpunished. But anyway...

MINAMORE   Interesting.

KENNEDY   We're not in El Salvador, but it's not far from the fact that residents from Grenfell took their complaints as far as they possibly could and didn't get anywhere because the state instruments that had previously provided oversight – the audit commission, the teeth that the housing ombudsman had previously had – had been taken away under a desire to decrease bureaucracy and give councils more power.

MAROŠEVIĆ   I think your car metaphor is a powerful one. What's interesting about housing in terms of its politics is that it doesn't actually take that long to build a set of houses, in the grand scheme of things. It's not like HS2 or other big infrastructure projects. In a way, it's an easy win for politicians.

BOUGHTON   I'll give you one practical reason why we might move positively in that direction, and that's the housing benefit bill. We spend £21 billion a year on housing benefit. What happened in the 80s was a shift from bricks and mortar subsidies, which is just what you've described, Željka, building homes, to personal allowances – basically paying housing benefit. In 1991 we paid £9 billion and at present rates it will be £70 billion by 2050. It's incredibly costly and financially ineffective. In comparison, investing in house building makes sense: social housing is not subsidised and never has been, and it pays for itself over the years.

'UNTIL IT TOUCHES EVERYONE.'

KENNEDY   There is something in the fact that: until it touches everyone, people do not understand it. Carolyn Forché again quotes Czeslaw Milosz to say: if a thing exists in one place, it will exist everywhere. So if discrimination is affecting one group of people in society, it can and will affect you at some point, either directly or indirectly. For me, that was what was so shocking about Grenfell, because you can't treat citizens in that way. And if our current legislative regime and elected representatives can treat one community in that way, they can treat any of us in that way. And they do.

MINAMORE   We've spoken a lot about London but I wanted to say that wherever you go in the country, the situation is just as bad if not worse. It's all so terrible. I could only have my career because I grew up in London, I can't imagine what it would have been like to be trying to get into the London-centric creative industries if I'd grown up on an estate in the middle of Hastings or Milton Keynes or County Durham. But I think one of the hopeful things is that the solutions are similar, whether you're in London or elsewhere in the country. It's about money and investment – and emotion.

BOUGHTON   If you go back to the very beginnings of social housing in the late nineteenth century, it happened for a number of reasons, including a certain amount of emotion and compassion, but what you had most of all was an absolute realisation across the political spectrum that private housing wouldn't solve the problem. And that's the single constant for me – the private market will not provide decent, secure, affordable housing in the numbers required. It's not designed to do so; it's not where its DNA lies. So council housing gets built because it has to be built, and I hope it will be in the future.

CHARLOTTE GEATER

POETRY

BANGABLE DUDES IN HISTORY

we collected together all of the scientists and historians & i said
okay, how about him.
he was a murderer – but it's
a photograph. sun in
his eyes. how many decades since
he tried it on?
we tried it on,

did we? we wouldn't do it, she said
& we took lifts from vans
on longwall street, pulled our tights up
from the waist, snacked outside libraries –
we needed headrushes
to punctuate our reading.

we salute you from new college's slippery mound
where we climbed to escape the tourists
& their guidebooks, laughing
at their own hands. we salute you
& your endeavours
noli me tangere, i am flying
i am flayed today – there are exams
& it is a good rotten apple summer, i think we bit away
the shade.

i spent so long reading reprinted old books that when i read
the new ones you told me about they said
oxford's problem is all the women

who won't fuck you – i thought
that's interesting. baby, did i make you sick?
the minstrels strummed
& we thumbed back through the pages – margins full of us.
this one's about anne boleyn & this one
is about wild game. the rhyme – it's so quiet.
noli me tangere, is it my right
to say that? i didn't like my legs
but didn't know what to wear
in case you saw them

& we spent lunches stuck on dead princes' faces.
this is not what you're like.
you only want to sing
about how much you love us anyway.

MORE URGENT & UNFORESEEN REASONS TO LOVE MYSELF
after 'The Fan' by Marie Laurencin

would i rather hold your fan
or fold myself into it?
gathered in & out again at my hidden parts
where dust/powder collects & your fingers
press down
who dares look at me so? who paints
the sky such violet & raw pink in early mornings?
who pinned a bow to my chest?
is this your dog left to my hands, shaking?
must i hold him while you dress?
must i bite my lip when you ask?
                                baby i don't have knees –
you gave me hard edges & you wonder
why i keep my distance.
a hairpin on the carpet
mascara pox on glass
cold dog kisses for my mouth
the night outside & in / fuzzy walls
of charcoal grey & black
& a starless sky, a canopy bed
i won't lie down for you
no fucking
tonight. & whose dog is this anyhow
your kisses blue / where have you been
a small box, very far away.
tissue paper. a few lines, scratched.
your puppy on his knees crying for you,
somewhere in the back. me, too.

THREE DAYS

so it's like, we shouldn't press our cheeks together
like we think / we know
because say i saw pen on my sock
this morning i looked and finally
let some noise pass through
lodge / into my ledgers,
take heart there
& i thought that there was something
in the words it slipped down but then all of this

my padded fingers slip on
to the handles swing above us
we are shifted i mean
shifting through
the undergrowth & i am

i have fallen over i slipped
#-#-#
yeah but it's fucking cheap they're all so frightened of him.
and i want some lemon drizzle & the pub & you

HERE. east oxford smells like cress now
burnt rubber snakes its way up st clements
smokes out the morning from my eyes
& now the day is rotten limes
in the way i speak to you, love

(####take heart, i never hit
the right keys))

so the notebook bloomed
when my cola leaked & i must wait
for it to dry. you try to make sense of it,
the brown from the red, i mean
but i can't see
that you're right.
all my thoughts come in full sentences.
i am trying to pretend
they do not. three weeks in muck &

three days away from you

they have nothing to do with what i mean?
but the radio, what men say, #hahaha
somebody lives there & kicks the ticker
when they should edit,
circle me deeper
they only know grammar, & even when you are waiting
we slip on my surfaces, talk for days
about how i should learn to eat again
with half a broken jaw & you will be here
when i sleep, three days from now

& the days past.

& i am always a gutted thing with hands
too cold still to work the phone.

THE BRICKLAYER'S ARMS

the pub kitchen / bobby pins
broke your crown

a clump of hair
oxtail soup the colour / bled your throat

we thickened the pudding with cornflour
there is no blue in your eyes / the after-image
we purged the soy / soaked you clean

dust rises from my tights
a fray at the knee

the university's drinking song

the earliest pies also functioned as

a mouldy ceiling / a broken lock
where do we live now / in dreams you brought
me round / broken nails off the sound

i mean / a graze so electric blue
how could i

a voice fit for public service
a coat dark enough to die in

the welt under your elbow turned yellow

the ashtrays glued in the perfect centre we assembled

a fairy's ring / my ear hidden beneath

when they turn the lights down and the music up

a plate of cold cuts / where i think your face is
from here only cat-eyes

the yellow gloom / the near-miss
dried red in long-dead light

MY FBI AGENT DOESN'T LIKE TO READ

but guess who is the other key member
of my radical book club!
i read a lot of ebooks because i am always thinking
of him
                     and his lack of access to an academic library
marxist monetary theory
kate millett's sexual politics
william morris biographies

am i teaching him to like
reading? to bend himself around
each line
i like to read
through his eyes
after i have read using mine or sometimes
when the tea brews right & my brain fires off
at speed
                   it ricochets back and folds in &
i can see each page twice at once
a small crease in the middle
two screens

one of us is prone on the ground
one of us is running
one of us is looping back around
one of us is lying
down

POETA EX MACHINA
for Veronica Forrest-Thomson

my voice makes the machine work
the tape clicks inside
but it's just ether now

if a voice is a long way away
and you are here, on paper
only it's like writing a maths

(a puzzle-box; i know
how better to move its body
when i move it with me)

problem – the voice animates
and if i animate the voice
and if what animates me is

scraping carrot cake off a wooden fork
with my teeth/tongue, reading you out
lying prone, saying loudly what

i want to repeat with myself
and also with my body
computing words / understanding through

gauze, and these little things
put away in boxes. stamps in thick ink.
i would like to hear your voice.

if what animates me is you.
if what animates the box is me.
and the different stories; each floor

is its own house, each room a world
with rules i can spend my whole life
playing a game with, looking for pain

& pleasure there. a string of tape with dots
in but the dots are holes. they mean things.
and the absences sing through clicking

and i scratch a diagram on the table.
and i would never speak for you.
still my body. puzzle-box. what old tape.

who knows that it's the power and the pain
the act of twisting one way / instead of staying
still that means: this is what meaning is

that it's grappling with a wall that makes
the house. that it's the torn nails. that it's
what hurts, and hurts badly. that the voice

rang out once, and will not again, but still.
still there is something that moves. that sets
the problem going. and somewhere / in the air

i would like to move, first. under my fingers
and running through my lungs: i wish you
were here too / is the solution. but not yet.

ENRIQUE VILA-MATAS INTERVIEW

In *Mac and his Problem*, Enrique Vila-Matas's latest novel, the author rejects originality, propos-
ing instead the figure of the ventriloquist as a model for a kind of literature that finds freshness
in the voice of another. Coming from one of the greatest innovators in world literature, this
proposal has a paradoxical ring to it, pointing towards the conceptual games and ironic displacements that Vila-Matas's readers have come to recognise as characteristic of his work. Starting
from his 1977 novel *La asesina ilustrada* (The Enlightened Murderess) - famously written from
Marguerite Duras's apartment, where he was boarding at the time, and composed with the
expressed intent of producing 'the death of the reader' – Vila-Matas's work has been defined by
its incessant exploration of what it could mean to be an avant-garde writer today. Alongside the
work of writers like Ricardo Piglia, Margo Glantz, Diamela Eltit and Sergio Pitol, his books
reimagine the hybridity inherent to literature, opening it in turn to the worlds of conceptual art
and philosophy. Literature as a space for the playfulness of thought: perhaps that could be a way
to define the poetics of an author whose claim to fame arrived in 1985 with the publication of
A Brief History of Portable Literature, a book that reimagined the history of the avant-garde from
the teasing perspective of a secret society called 'the Shandies', whose members included Marcel
Duchamp, Witold Gombrowicz and Walter Benjamin, and whose aim was the proposal of
a literature devoid of heaviness and severity. Vila-Matas has remained faithful to this proposal
ever since, producing some of the most influential books of recent decades, including his 2000
Bartleby & Co., a novel which, adopting Herman Melville's eponymous character and his famous
phrase 'I would prefer not to', rewrites the history of literature from the lens of writers who one
day adopted silence as their private art. In the books that followed – *Montano's Malady*, *Never Any
End to Paris* and *Dublinesque* – he continued to rewrite this secret history of literature in ways that
would profoundly transform the way we read: Robert Walser, Witold Gombrowicz, Marguerite
Duras and James Joyce would never be the same after his interventions, nor artists like Marcel
Duchamp or Man Ray. It should not surprise, then, that his work has recently jumped frontiers
and that his latest books – *Illogic of Kassel* or *Because She Never Asked* – work as art projects in
themselves, usually as collaborations with artists such as Sophie Calle or Dominique Gonzalez-
Foerster. For in his work, as this interview shows, what is at stake is always that fragile frontier
that separates literature from conceptual art and conceptual art from thought. All of these false
frontiers Vila-Matas destroys with his well-known audacity and irony. That is to say, with his
literary bravery and humour. CARLOS FONSECA

THE WHITE REVIEW   I'd like to start by talking about your beginnings as a writer. We come across several origin myths in your work, like the one where you pretended to be mad at the age of twenty-three in order to escape military service in Melilla and ended up writing your first book from the backroom of an African store, or the anecdote about how you wrote *La asesina ilustrada* from Marguerite Duras's Paris loft apartment. How do you view these multiple beginnings today?

ENRIQUE VILA-MATAS   I think we're talking about a universal law: one meets one's destiny in the most trivial, the most futile places of all. In my case, my destiny as a writer was waiting for me behind the door of that store in Melilla, where – in order to feel that I wasn't wasting too much time, as I had a year of colonial military service in Africa ahead of me – I began writing a poetic monologue, which I called a 'novel' in order to make it clearer in my head, but which was actually subject entirely to the laws of poetry, the only ones I knew back then as I'd barely read anything else. It was a monologue on the subject of anything and everything that freely inspired me. Automatic writing. I don't think there was anything wrong with the method I used for my first book, quite the opposite in fact. At the end of the day, as J.M. Coetzee has said, one of the things people don't usually understand about writers is that one doesn't start by having something to write about and then writing about it; rather, it's the actual process of writing itself that allows the author to discover what it is they want to say.

I'd simply written it in order to feel like I was doing something out there, not just vegetating – I suddenly began to think of myself as a writer, and I went to Paris with the idea of having a life like the one Hemingway describes in *A Moveable Feast*. In an episode destined for a future novel I did in fact end up writing, I met Marguerite Duras the moment I arrived, and she let me rent out one of her loft apartments. And that's how it all started, and I'd talk about some of the things that happened there years later in *Never Any End to Paris*.

TWR   You open *Never Any End to Paris* with a wonderful scene where you tell the story of how you travelled to Florida to sign up for the long-established Ernest Hemingway lookalike competition. These *mises-en-scene* occur throughout your work, where the writer appears both as a character and as an actor. It's as if you're countering the dull figure of the engaged writer with the image of the multiplicitous, ironic, evasive writer...

EVM   In my youth, I'd traverse the whole of Barcelona by night, staying at parties until the crack of dawn. As I took leave of my friends I'd say (with great conviction): 'I'm off then, bye. By the way, did you know I've given up writing?' And they all made it clear to me that what I was saying made no sense, because I didn't write anyway. When I remember these farewell scenes (I was reminded of this by a graphic novel on the subject of the Barcelona nightlife of that period, which once more put those words, so frequently uttered in those days, back into my mouth), I realise that long before I actually wrote, I wanted to *stop writing*. I realise too that the poetics of wanting to give up writing (an engaged writer, I think, feels this temptation to stop writing less) was what eventually made me become a writer.

TWR   *A Brief History of Portable Literature* was perhaps your first book to achieve the status of literary myth. In it, you tell the story of the Shandy society, an imagined group composed of members whose complete works must be portable, and who must behave like bachelor machines, living irreverent, nomadic lives. What was the significance of that book for you?

EVM   I believe the initial idea for the book came from an exhibition about *machines célibataires* (Marcel Duchamp's expression) that I saw in 1983, at the Grand Palais in Paris. I was intrigued by the title of that show alone: I didn't know you could put on a whole exhibition about 'bachelor machines'. At the time I was a great admirer of Raymond Roussel's 1914 novel *Locus Solus*, and I was deeply affected by seeing the imaginary machines he had described actually on display there, even more so because they were exhibited next to machines invented by Kafka (the one from the Penal Colony, for example) or Duchamp. I also liked the very concept of the *machine célibataire*, and completely identified with it. When I returned to Barcelona, I wrote an article about celibate machines, a ludicrous article published in *La Vanguardia*, which eventually became the origin of my book about the Shandy conspiracy. *A Brief History* was published in Spain in 1985, where it was poorly received because narrative fiction was dominated at the time by a trend known as 'anti-experimentalism', a movement which positioned itself against 'the avant-garde excesses of the 1970s'. But in Mexico the book was reviewed twenty-seven times in less than three weeks, and it was adored in France and Italy. Something had been put in motion. In fact, in Sweden the book was the inspiration for the journal *Ankan* (of which there were two issues), which called itself 'Europe's first *Shandy* magazine'. Basically, things began happening for me. An Argentine critic, for example, said that I'd written a 'radical work of fiction'. And I had not intended to make something like that, all I knew was that I was dedicated to the art of fiction, but I didn't know what the hell this 'radical' thing meant. Hadn't Vladimir Nabokov said that 'fiction is fiction', which reminds me of Oscar Wilde in *Salomé*: 'The moon is the moon, nothing more'?

TWR   And speaking of Nabokov, you've mentioned in several texts his belief that the most interesting thing in a writer's biography isn't 'the chronicle of his adventures' but 'the history of his style'. There is, without doubt, a Vila-Matas style. Yet in your last novel, *Mac and his Problem*, you pursue the idea that originality does not exist and that all writing is re-writing. What does style signify for you nowadays?

EVM   When I witness a heavyweight dialectical confrontation between two intelligent people I tend to agree with everything one of them says, and then also with everything the other one says, regardless of the extent to which what one of them says is the total opposite of what the other has said. I think that on the one hand, this indicates that my spirit is very open and that I can accept two ideas, however contradictory they may be. (Walt Whitman: 'Do I contradict myself? Very well, then I contradict myself. I am large, I contain multitudes.') On the other hand, it indicates that in reality I tend not to believe in anything, not to have faith in anything, as Plato advised. It's impossible for me to believe in originality, no matter how conscious I am of the existence of a Vila-Matas style. However, having created this style doesn't make me an original writer. As Josep Pla used to say, nothing is more disagreeable than sterile, useless attempts to arrive at a wild and primitive style.

My style nowadays? It's dictated by the way my work has unfolded. In *Mac* I dedicated myself to rewriting *Una casa para siempre* (A House Forever), the 1988 novel in which, paradoxically, I established my style by questioning the very idea that a writer is nothing if he doesn't have his own voice. That style was born, then, from the idea that a novel must be constructed in opposition to a popular place or idea from the era in which it is written: this is what I had seen happening in *Don Quixote*, and consequently in *Tristram Shandy*, where Lawrence Sterne uses John Locke's doctrines – theories about how to write novels without falling victim to the 'association of ideas' which the English philosopher considered dangerous – to make it look like he is adhering to them, when really he is doing so in the most ironic way possible. All of *Tristram Shandy* is actually a hugely ironic revolt against Locke's theories of literary moderation, it laughs in their face.

I think that many of the novels I've written have tended to go against an idea or theory, against the idea (or the counter-idea) which had guided the writing of my previous novel. Perhaps my style, as far as it exists, is most frequently characterised by my allowing the work to unfold, to be carried along while I simultaneously critique the work in question.

TWR   You've mentioned elsewhere that reading *Tristram Shandy* was one of the great events in your life. What do you remember about that first reading? What is it about this book that you consider to be contemporary?

EVM   I read *Tristram Shandy* in Spanish, in Javier Marías's translation, which was accompanied by some highly memorable 'Notes', which I remember as being absolutely superlative. I found the book extraordinarily free and entertaining, razor-sharp, especially in the relationship between the author and the reader. I see now that in that copy of *Tristram Shandy*'s combination of notes and narrative lay the nucleus of some of the books I would go on to write, where fiction and essay complement each other organically.

TWR   Your work seems to be written, in the words of that other great reader of Sterne, Machado de Assis, in his prologue to *The Posthumous Memoirs of Bras Cubas* (aka *Epitaph of a Small Winner*), with 'playful pen and melancholy ink'...

EVM   When I began to write, I did so in a country where I felt no one was doubting anything, and where, because nobody was allowed to doubt anything anyway, you had to be in agreement with the Guiding Lights of the era, to stand to attention before them. Then I discovered the pleasures of dissidence. And as time passed, after years of discreet but effective infractions, of novels that went against one idea or another, and always against my previous novel, I became familiar with a scene in the life of the young Witold Gombrowicz that summed up the way I had been in my first flush of youth, and how my literary discourse had subsequently formed: 'The sun is shining, my mother would say. No, I'd say, it's raining. You're always saying silly things, she'd say. OK, I'd say, let's say it's not raining, but if it started to rain, it would be raining, and I'd become melancholy. I'd drag her into absurd discussions, and it was with her that I first took up the exercise of dialectic and critique.'

TWR   Your desire to somehow rewrite the story of the avant-garde movement – from Duchamp to Federico García Lorca, from Walter Benjamin to Tristan Tzara – has ended up becoming one of your recurring themes. Why do you envisage your own fiction from this starting point?
EVM   When I was very young, I saw Duchamp playing chess in Cadaqués, in Bar Melitón. I witnessed him losing a game, and I'd never seen anyone lose with such elegance and dignity. Years later I found a book about him, which made a great impression on me. The book was *Dialogues with Marcel Duchamp* by Pierre Cabanne, where Duchamp says: 'I understood, at a certain moment, that it wasn't necessary to encumber one's life with too much weight, with too many things to do, with what is called a wife, children, a country house, an automobile, etc.' In a way, that book showed me what a good path for an independent artist looked like, and I think I ended up using it almost like a self-help book, before those idiotic things became fashionable. The truth is that in contrast with Francoist, bourgeois Barcelona, living in Cadaqués was like living abroad, always surrounded by avant-garde artists. Even Boris Vian's widow, who was around there at the time, had a 'dadaist' air about her. You'd often see artists like Man Ray, John Cage, Richard Hamilton... My cultural formation may well have begun in that Catalan village on the French border.

TWR   Back then you wanted to be a filmmaker, if I remember correctly. How did you make the transition from cinema to literature?
EVM   Through circumstance. The circumstances in question were the year of military service I've already talked about: a year in North Africa with no leave, which meant that I couldn't work on anything cinema-related, and which led me to write a semi-poetic monologue in the little spare time I had, in the afternoons in that store in Melilla. And it was highly fortunate that circumstance did lead me to this fate, because there wasn't the slightest hope of me having any future in cinema. I was greatly influenced by the underground cinema of the 1960s: Jonas Mekas, Philippe Garrel, Glauber Rocha, Adolfo Arrietta, and others. And because I refused to make any concessions whatsoever to the world of 'commercial cinema' (which I passionately despised), I ended up having no chance of finding a producer anywhere. In Cadaqués I'd directed *Summer's End*, a short film produced by my father. When I first showed the film, at a screening for my friends, the film was met with incomprehension by everyone apart from my father, to whom it was quite clear what the film was all about. 'If I'm not mistaken,' he said to me, 'the theme is the destruction of the bourgeois family.' At that moment I understood that I'd lost the only producer available to me, and that a long desert crossing awaited me. And so my call-up to the army – which certainly brought me very close to the Sahara desert – ended up being providential for me.

TWR   You've often surrounded yourself with Latin American authors. I'm thinking about the work of authors like Roberto Bolaño, Ricardo Piglia, and your friend Sergio Pitol, whom you have mentioned was the first to treat you as if you were really a writer.
EVM   You've just named three of the writers I've followed and admired the most, and with whom I've had the best personal relationships. I met all three in similar circumstances: on the street, while walking towards a restaurant, we began talking about literature – Bolaño in Blanes, Pitol in Warsaw, and Piglia in Puerto de Santa María.

TWR   Sergio Pitol died just a few days ago. How do you remember him?
EVM   Pitol has been called a 'rare, secret classic', and I think that's a very good way of describing him. I especially recommend *The Art of Flight* to the English-language reader. It's the most incredible discovery. As to how I remember him, I have an infinite number of memories, but basically, they are ones that will be forever kept alive by laughter

and happiness. However there is one moment from all my memories of Pitol that I would highlight above all others. It wasn't exactly a Borgesian moment, at which I knew who I really was from that point on, but it did make me realise the things he was capable of in his writing, the sort of verbal somersaults he managed to bring to life. Because I feel like I can still hear the master, that morning at his house in Xalapa, Mexico, some quarter of a century ago, a few hours after I had risked my life in the night of Veracruz, and he couldn't believe I was still laughing, and I can still feel myself there watching the way he, to my great surprise and using only words, moved suddenly from happiness and light to darkness in what appeared to me – in an incredible incursion of literature into life – to be a smooth technical display of the kind he employed in *Nocturno de Bujara*, where he moves from narrative to essay without anyone noticing.

TWR   In *Bartleby & Co*, which takes its name from Melville's famous story, you weave a great constellation of writers of the No: writers who one day feel the pull of nothingness, and decide to stop writing. Have you ever felt yourself attracted by this negative pull?

EVM   I think I wrote it precisely because I did feel that negative pull, and I adopted the strategy of writing about those who became paralysed and stopped writing, in order not to give up writing myself. Duchamp's famous urinal, for example, is a negation of art, and at the same time it is a step towards another way of viewing the phenomenon of art. There is, in these negations of sculpture, of literature, a very strong passion for that which is being denied.

TWR   Ricardo Piglia said that *Discourse on the Method* was the first modern novel because it narrated 'the passion for an idea'. I think this sentence is also an apt description of your work.

EVM   What you're saying seems to fit in with our discussion about the novel as an idea that goes against another established idea. Piglia is one of the writers I've most enjoyed reading, perhaps because his whole body of work is an inexhaustible succession of incessant, open answers to the question of what is and what isn't literature. I can't forget how, as I was finishing *Mac*, he reminded me that fiction in Europe comes from the Arabs. It was as if he had guessed where my character, Mac, was going (towards the Orient), and what the meaning of my

novel was: an attempt at orientation.

TWR   Together with *Doctor Pasavento* and *Montano's Malady*, *Bartleby & Co* forms part of a trilogy in which negativity plays a central part, and where, as Robert Walser outlined, writing is always a model of disappearance. Thinking about the cases of Arthur Cravan, Hart Crane or Ambrose Bierce, all of whom disappeared, do you believe the fate of the avant-garde to be one of mythical disappearance?

EVM   One of my favourite characters is Bobi Bazlen, a Turin native and a legendary figure from the world of Italian publishing, whom I discovered in Daniele del Giudice's novel *Lo stadio di Wimbledon*. He was one of the first to say that books could no longer be written. I think that in this trilogy (*Bartleby, Montano, Pasavento*), where negativity is central, I turned that negation up a notch. The power of disenchantment – the feeling that it's no longer possible to write books – makes the work of art stronger and, paradoxically, more vulnerable.

TWR   I like that, 'the power of disenchantment'. And it makes me think that any given genre only recognises its vanguard in the exact moment at which the other genre threatens to replace it: the novel threatened by cinema, painting by photography, cinema by television. It's as if the artform in question, liberated from the responsibility of representing what is real, can finally begin to rant and rave. A liberating threat that in some way halts the decline of your work...

EVM   I couldn't be more delighted with the potential of what you are saying. The novel, faced with a severe existential threat, finally discovers its own essence. Didn't Blanchot already address this perfectly?

TWR   Nevertheless, the beauty of your work lies in how it manages to sketch a possible way back from that initial act of disappearance. In a way this return was already being mapped out in *Montano's Malady*. And I'll venture to say that, after its initial act of disappearance, the avant-garde comes back not just as a story but as a way of life. Just as the protagonist of *Montano's Malady* chooses to make the history of literature flesh, your subsequent novels are given over to the task of embodying the proposals outlined by the same avant-garde whose disappearance you had described. To some extent this is your way of continuing to make literature beyond the end of literature, what you call – in your novel *Dublinesque* - the end of the Gutenberg Era. In fact, the theme of the end, of the abyss, is a constant in your literature. How do you envisage these endings, and how do you manage to keep moving forward?

EVM From the time of *Bartleby & Co* (2000) onwards, finishing a book began to mean, for me, having taken the obsession that had moved me to write it to the limit, then arriving at the end of a cul-de-sac and having to ask myself how I would manage to keep going. That was also what my friends were asking me: 'What are you going to do now? How will you keep going?' I decided I would try to lead all my books into that cul-de-sac, and at the same time I decided to have a sentence from Adolfo Bioy Casares as my companion for moving on from each book, that is to say, moving on from that cul-de-sac. The sentence is: 'Intelligence is the art of finding a tiny hole through which to get out of the situation we are trapped in.' So one could say that I have of late – for at least fifteen years – been working with one method: taking everything to the limits of obsession, and of the abyss, and then finding the way out, if only because finding it means continuing to write.

TWR Now I think of it, your art is one of limits and of obsession, the poetics of a fixed idea. Have you ever feared, like Machado de Assis's characters, that fixed ideas may ultimately lead to madness?

EVM Not at all. The most that could happen is that I would one day find myself in a high-up place, looking down on the world from above.

TWR That coming back, or continuation of literature beyond its ending, is somehow linked in your work with a clear shift towards a world that has always been present in your books: the world of art, specifically conceptual art. I'm thinking of your collaborations with Sophie Calle or Dominique Gonzalez-Foerster, and of books like *The Illogic of Kassel*. How do you view the connection between art and literature?

EVM I'm someone who believes that the legacy of the modernists has ended up finding its most prominent place in the visual arts. Joyce's works, for example, have sparked the interest of people working in fields far beyond the confines of literature, especially in the worlds of art and science. The dynamism, and the capacity for renovation present in the literature of the first half of the last century, have been inherited by the world of art, where I can see a greater malleability, a restlessness, and a sharper perception of global issues. The thing is, editorial power is forever held hostage to the logic of the market. I've been most pleased by the reception which a book like *The Illogic of Kassel* has had in the restless world of contemporary art, and I think it has opened up unexplored spaces in literature. As Chus Martínez, who curated Documenta in Kassel in 2012, said: '*The Illogic of Kassel* is the first novel about an exhibition.'

TWR Speaking of Joyce, in *Dublinesque* you constructed a kind of funeral for literature and the Gutenberg era around the figures of Joyce and Samuel Beckett, framed within the Bloomsday celebrations. What do you think the legacy of that memorable pair of writers, so similar and yet so different, has been?

EVM Their literary spectres project themselves over the writers whom I consider to be the best working in narrative fiction today, but I won't name any names, as it's a complex undertaking. I think that in order to understand the relationship between Beckett and Joyce, you have to pay attention to the moment at which Beckett realises that he has to do away with the malign influence of his teacher, when he writes the following to his friend Thomas McGreevy: 'Joyce was sublime last night, deprecating with the utmost conviction his lack of talent. I don't feel the danger of the association any more. He is just a very lovable human being.'

TWR Don DeLillo often remarks that 'writing is a concentrated form of thinking'.

EVM That's a great saying of DeLillo's. It's something Nietzsche could have said.

TWR Which leads me to another quote that could have been uttered by Borges: 'All of literature is play.' Your work always plays around with apocryphal or misplaced quotations. Do you remember where your passion for playing with quotations came from?

EVM It came from the films of Jean-Luc Godard (which I used to watch in the 1970s) and later from Edgardo Cozarinsky, who in his wonderful book *Urban Voodoo* made use of quotations in what Susan Sontag identified as being a Godardian fashion. And also, it barely needs mentioning, from Sterne. If I remember correctly, when Sterne spoke of 'shutting the study door', what he really meant was that he wished to distance himself from the authors in his library whose work he tended to copy. In fact, one of Sterne's most famous fragments can be read as a blistering assault on authors who plagiarise, and an attempt by Sterne himself to make amends by proclaiming that he will never copy again. But perhaps the most brilliant thing about that fragment is that it is itself plagiarised from Robert Burton's *Anatomy of Melancholy*, that great book that would always come to his mind, dutifully and punctually, when he was feeling somewhat dejected.

There has been a constant process of evolution in my relationship with facts. In the last few years I've begun to go deeper into this territory. Far from stopping quoting (which was tempting, as quoting was sometimes wrongly viewed by my enemies as a weak point in my narrative, and therefore a side of me that was open to attack), I preferred to insist on this approach and to start investigating why it was that I quoted so much, and whether or not there was a meaning to this which I had yet to discover, like figuring out why, over time, I had ended up inventing the majority of my quotations. In some way the art of quoting was gradually becoming a strong point in my writing, especially from the moment I discovered that Georges Perec, one of my favourite writers, could act as my alibi, for he had been a keen practitioner of this art. Already in 1965, not long after he published *Things*, Perec had displayed a great sense of optimism by saying that literature was on its way to becoming an *citational art*, an artform that could be seen as progressive if one bore in mind that the artist-quoter took as his starting point everything our predecessors considered to be a notable achievement, an interesting discovery... My insistence on upholding this enigmatic path, the mania for quoting, has led me to my recent creation of the character of Bastian Schneider, distributor of quotations, the subaltern of an author whom he feeds with stray sentences. In the novel I'm writing, where he plays a considerable part, that art of citation is the crux of the story. In it, Schneider tries to create a bizarre archive of quotations which he hopes to bring together in an encyclopaedia-cum-vault he wants one day to show in public – wide open, with every index card visible – in a window display in the centre of Barcelona. His idea is to carry out a Benjaminian work of criticism in a shopping centre: the arduous chore of showing the immense weight of all the hot air and nonsense in the world; the scandalous and banal nature, immensely eloquent in its general imbecility, of the infinite charlatanism contained in every era.

TWR   You've said that of all your fabrications, your books are the most truthful: 'I've always been concealing myself, leaving red herrings everywhere, while at the same time offering up unsettling aspects of my different personalities, all of them true, to the reader.' Where does Enrique Vila-Matas sit in this theatre of truths and fabrications?
EVM   In recent years I've come to believe that I do know who I am, perhaps because I am the same age as Don Quixote, who in the midst of his hallucinations shouted: 'I know who I am.' I'm someone who is dedicated to the art of fiction, and who thinks that the most attractive thing about literature is the way it unsettles us by placing the question of language and representation in plain sight; it makes us realise that language isn't something that represents reality, but rather something that both makes reality, and undoes it. It manages this from the position of a decisive, unassailable subjectivity, which, I believe, brings with it a moral charge, and a radical aesthetics. This turns conventional novels into mere commercial products, making them akin to dishwasher tablets which – please excuse the note of humour – nowadays people actually chew – they eat them – for no reason other than because it's fashionable.

C. F., translated by Rahul Bery,
May 2018

MAGNETISED

A CONVERSATION WITH RICARDO MELOGNO

CARLOS BUSQUED
tr. SAMUEL RUTTER

The following text is the condensed result of over ninety hours of dialogue with Ricardo Melogno, recorded between November 2014 and December 2015. The conversations were much longer and more disparate, and the topics were covered with less continuity and greater chaos than in the current text. My edits respect the words of the interviewee while compressing, grouping and organising them chronologically and thematically, with the goal of providing structure to his story. I believe I have respected the concepts expounded by Ricardo, but I take full responsibility for any differences or mistakes arising from the editing process. C. B.

TURNING TOWARDS THE DARKNESS

'I was told that someone saw you levitate.'
[*Melogno furrows his brow, smiles with amusement.*]
'Who?'
'Someone who knew you from Unit 20 and was convicted again. They brought him here and when he saw you, he asked to be kept as far away from you as possible. He said that you were evil, and that he had seen you levitate.'
'Oh, I know who that is, ha ha... Well, you see, that kid's real impressionable. Among other major issues he has.

Here's the thing with me. Inside the prison, things pass from mouth to mouth and they start adding up. Over the years it's sort of snowballed. Even now, when they send in the search parties (they're not guards from here, but from the 'regular' prison, and they come every two or three months) they find the shrine in my cell with all the offerings and the candles, they say: 'Old man, what are you into here? What's all this strange stuff?' But these guys are more modern these days, they ask more out of curiosity, not out of fear.

[*On his left arm he has a tattoo with three symbols on top of each other: at the top is a 666, in the middle an inverted crucifix and on the bottom a reversed swastika. The line of symbols is flanked by two snakes writhing rampantly from left to right.*]
'Why the reversed swastika?'
'The regular swastika, the one used by the Nazis, represents turning towards the sun, towards the light. So I got mine tattooed like this, turning towards the darkness.'
'Who gave you this tattoo?'
'I did it myself, watching my arm in a mirror.'
'Why do you pray to the devil?'
'Because I feel him.'
'Doesn't the devil inspire evil deeds?'
'If that's what I thought, I'd be a Christian. Evil comes from within a person, not from religion. Just because someone has a dark side doesn't necessarily mean they're evil in their life. The idea that because I worship Satan, I must be a son of a bitch, is a Christian idea. It's like saying that the youth has turned to shit because they listen to rock and roll. Youth turns to shit for a thousand other reasons, but not because of rock and roll.'

YOUTH TURNED TO SHIT

In September 1982, a series of brief, strange and almost restrained murders took place in the city of Buenos Aires. Over the course of one week, in an area spanning no more than a few blocks in the neighbourhood of Mataderos, the lifeless bodies of four taxi drivers were found. Each of the corpses appeared in the early hours of the morning, slumped forward in the front seats of their taxis, with a .22 calibre bullet hole in the right temple. The taxis were parked on dark corners, with their interior lights and engines switched off, and their headlights ablaze. There was no sign of robbery, although registration documents for the vehicles and ID for the victims were missing. Except for the last incident, the taxi meters all read zero.

Only three of the four murders made the news: on 24 September, the *La Razón, Crónica, La Prensa* and *Clarín* newspapers laid out the discovery of the body of A. R. on the corner of Pola and Basualdo Streets in a few lines. Four days later, slightly more space was dedicated to the discovery of C. C., on the 1800 block of Oliden Street. The individual in question was not yet dead, but he was dying. He had a hole in his skull that was bleeding profusely, and in the end, he died on the way to the hospital. Following this second incident, the 42nd Precinct organised a sweeping operation, swarming Mataderos with their own officers as well as reinforcements from the Robbery and Assault, Crime Prevention and Investigations Units. Despite all this deployment, on 28 September the body of J. G. was found on the corner of Basualdo and Tapalqué streets, only 400 metres from the other bodies. Later, two more incidents (thwarted holdups of taxis) took place in the same area, in which the drivers received wounds from blunt objects but emerged relatively unscathed. One of the drivers gave a description of his attacker, which was mocked up into an identikit and disseminated through the newspapers and television.

Police were unable to shed light on the crimes. The only certainties gathered by the agents of order? That all the crimes were the work of a single individual, and that during the attacks, the perpetrator had not moved from the rear seat of the taxi.

The void left by the lack of progress in the investigation was filled, in the Buenos Aires media, with hypotheses of varying degrees of craziness: 'We cannot rule out the possibility that this psychopath is a woman in disguise, with very short hair'; 'The murderer might be a student attending night school who is mentally unstable and attacks taxi drivers after class'; 'The maniac called the 42nd Precinct and vowed to attack again, insisting that nobody could stop him'; 'The murderer is a psychopath with a complex personality, it is thought that he kills only on the corners of streets whose names have an even number of letters in them.' Taxi drivers began attacking passengers they thought resembled the identikit. In several sweeps, the police detained over twenty 'persons of interest' who turned out to have nothing to do with the crimes.

On the morning of 15 October, a man presented himself at the Palace of Tribunals in the Federal Capital and asked to speak with the judge presiding over the case. He said he was coming to 'clear his name'. The taxi murderer was his brother, who at that very moment was with their father, having breakfast in an apartment in Caballito. He offered to take the police there. He assured the judge that his brother was unarmed and that they would be able to arrest him without incident.

The mysterious murderer turned out to be twenty years old, and he looked completely different to the identikit. His name was Ricardo Luis Melogno.

During the judicial interrogation, the young man admitted to the three murders, but denied having committed the two attacks without fatalities. The surviving taxi drivers did not identify him as the culprit.

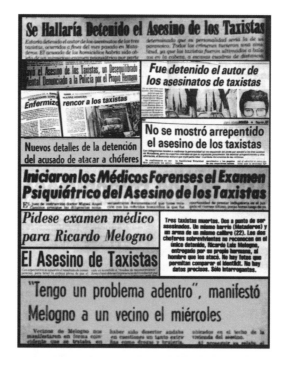

He confessed to another murder in Lomas del Mirador, close to Mataderos but on the other side of General Paz Avenue, outside the city limits of Buenos Aires. When the police from the Province of Buenos Aires were consulted, they confirmed that a taxi driver, with a surname of T—, had recently been found murdered in identical conditions to the previous three. In fact, those three weren't previous but subsequent murders. Chronologically, that fourth crime was actually the first.

A PROBLEM INSIDE

Apparently, the suspect's father was the first to find evidence, when he discovered the victims' identity documents, which his son guarded jealously. While many minor details remain unknown, it's clear that the anguished father asked for advice from his other son, and together they arrived at the conclusion that they should deliver Ricardo Luis to justice.

In the paternal home, a .22 calibre pistol was found.

Ricardo Luis Melogno was interrogated for six hours, during which time he readily confessed to the crimes and was examined by forensic doctors. Throughout the investigation he was observed to be calm, without ever showing signs of nerves. When he was asked why he committed the crimes, he refused to answer.

Neighbours in the area agreed on a description of the young man as timid and withdrawn, who clearly concealed a horrifying tangle of feelings and impulses beneath a calm surface. They also said that Ricardo sometimes left the house in his military service uniform. He was discharged from the military, but had extra time added to his service as a punishment for having lost or stolen weapons of war on the grounds of the Villa Martelli Army Barracks, located on Avenida General Paz, between Tejar and Constituyentes Streets.

'His father was well regarded in the neighbourhood, and concerning his mother, it was said that she lived at a different abode, apparently in a shantytown.

One neighbour, who did not wish to give his name, said that on occasions he had come across Ricardo acting strangely, standing still in one place, lost in his thoughts, his eyes fixed to the ground.'

Clarín, 17 October 1982

'According to statements gathered, he is a strange young man, with obvious psychological problems. He was described as very shy and withdrawn, with few links to his neighbours, whom he mostly ignored, along with other young people of his own age. 'He's very taciturn, not the type to strike up conversation.' For the last few months he had been living in a room at the back of his father's house, detached from the main building.

His strange personality moved the magistrate assigned to the case to call for psychiatric and psychological examinations to be undertaken in the coming hours, to determine if Melogno's mental characteristics are normal.'

La Razón, 18 October 1982

'Throughout the interrogation Melogno responded in detail to questions asked by the judge, but he remained consistently mute whenever he was asked why he had committed the crimes. He never stole a dime. So what was the motive for the chilling executions? Silence was the only answer.

There seem to be few concrete facts about his life. No one knows where to find his father or brother. It is as if the ground has swallowed them up. No relatives have come forward, nor anyone who can provide a photograph of Ricardo Luis Melogno. Where is the mother? That remains unknown. Just one more unanswered question to add to the many others that have prevented us from reconstructing the life of a murderer who is barely twenty years old.'

Revista Gente, the week after the arrest

'Without admitting to friendship or regular contact, a neighbour indicated that he regularly spoke with Melogno, and that he didn't seem like an imbalanced individual. "The only time I saw him looking strange was Wednesday, when we passed each other on the street. When I saw the desperate look on his face, I asked him what was wrong, and he said 'I have a problem inside.' But I have no idea what he meant by the word 'inside.'"'

La Prensa, 18 October 1982

BAPTISED IN BLOOD

I had a dog, a Pomeranian crossed with something else, that I found in the street. I wanted to call her Benji (it was around the time the film *Benji* came out) but in the end she was called Juana, because my mother said: 'She's going to be called Juana.' She used to call me 'Juana' as well. She called the three of us brothers 'girls'. She accepted my bringing the dog home, but she treated her very poorly. She would beat the dog with the same stick she used to beat us. And that thing I told you about how all men are botched abortions? That came from one time when my mother was beating the dog and my eldest brother tried to defend her. That's when my mother came out with it: all men are botched abortions.

Later, there was a cat, the poor thing... I was pretty nasty to that cat.

Because of all the problems I got into at school, at one point my mother sent me to live with this sort of boyfriend she had, who was a doorman at the Hotel Rawson. That's the hotel I told you about where I went to see about jumping off the roof. That all happened when I was living there.

Why did she do that?

What?

Send you to live with someone else?

Because of all the shit around sending me to school. I think they knew each other through religion, the guy was a spiritualist too, someone from the same part of the countryside as her. Opposite the hotel there was a Catholic school, and the boyfriend sent me there during the week and I went home to my mother's place on the weekends.

So, my mother brought this cat home. Then the cat began to take my place. My mother had it castrated. The cat took my spot, the son of a bitch. So, whenever I went home, I would torture the cat as much as I could. I'd put it in the freezer. Or I'd grab it by the scruff of the neck, its legs dangling in the air, and then I'd pull its tongue while I yanked its head the other way. Things like that. The poor cat was terrified of me. As soon as he saw me he'd dash off to hide on the roof. Afterwards he couldn't get down, he'd climb the walls and stay up there mewling, and then the only way to get him down was with a ladder, a real fucking mess.

That's when my mother put a collar on him, along with a leash, and at the end of the leash she attached a roller-bearing this big (*Melogno makes a circle 20cm in diameter with his hands*) so that he couldn't get away. The cat spent his life dragging that heavy roller-bearing around. You'd know the cat was nearby from the sound of the roller-bearing being dragged along, or because he got tangled around the legs of the furniture. And imagine that, from all that time dragging the bearing along, the cat's legs grew massive. He looked like some kind of beast.

I don't know what happened afterwards to the cat. When I left home my mother gave the dog away. I know she went to a good home. But I don't know what happened to the cat.

And where did that cat come from? Did she find it?

No, she bought it.

So, what you're saying is, as soon as you left home, your mother bought a cat, had it castrated and then tied it to a roller-bearing that weighed two kilos?

Yeah. You see my mother had this sort of perverse obsession with ownership and control.

I wasn't allowed to have friends, and no one could come and visit me either, because according to her, anyone from outside could hurt me. As I got a little older, I began to see a future where she was grooming me to be the submissive son who cares for her in her old age.

Once we were at my godmother's place, an apartment in the city centre. She was a nurse at the Borda Hospital and she was a spiritualist too. The two old ladies went out, who knows what they were up to, and I was left with my godmother's son, who must have been, let's say, twenty-five years old. After a while a girl he works with came over, because they had something they had to do, a work thing, nothing strange. I just sat there in silence, without interfering, while they chatted. A few hours went by and the old ladies came back, and my godmother started asking her son who this girl was, why she was there. So he started explaining and then the old lady cut him off and said 'I told you never to bring anyone here!' Then she slapped him across the face. Right in front of the girl. This was a defining moment in my adolescence. I saw that and my immediate thought was: if this sucker is still getting slapped around at twenty-five years of age, what's going to happen to me? And I said to myself: I'm getting out of here, no matter what.

To get free of my mother, I began to study Santería.

The thing is, when it came to my mother, apart from physical fear, I also had this religious fear. I tried to gain knowledge in spiritualism to get one over on my mother. But even my mother's spiritualist friends told me: 'You're crazy, you'll never get anywhere like this.' But there were others who had the clarity to tell me: 'Look, we'll set you on this other path and you'll be fine.' So, they sent me to Brazil and I entered into Santería. But I never did it because of faith, I did it as a tool to fight my mother. I needed strength to confront her.

How old were you around this time?

Thirteen, fourteen years old.

And how were these people connected to your mother?

They were friends through her religion, other spiritualists. There was some contact between spiritualism and Santería, they were two sides of the same coin, in certain respects.

Why did you have to go to Brazil?

Because there's no Santería in Argentina. I spent nearly a month in Buzios. I went to meetings, I joined the cult. I was baptised in blood. I made ground.

What does 'make ground' mean?

Santería is not like those evangelical churches where you rock up, you say 'I accept Jesus Christ' and right there and then they dip you in the water to baptise you and it's all done. With Santería, I spent several days in a completely dark room, spread out on the floor, to purify myself. In the initiation process for Santería it's not the group of people who have to accept you. The spirits have to accept you: you are presented before them, and just as easily as they can accept you, they can also reject you, and bounce you off the walls. I was baptised in blood. They gave me my patron saints, the ones who would guide me and give me strength.

What type of blood was it?

Blood from a black rooster. They hold it above your head when they kill it, so the blood runs over you.

Do they give you a new name during the initiation?

No. They give you your patron saints. A spirit can accept you and help you, but if not, it can treat you really bad.

And who speaks to you?

The spirits take control of the *pai*, a kind of priest, and speak to you.

Did the spirits speak to you?

Yes. But I couldn't understand a thing, it was some ancient language.

Does the trance produce any physical changes in a person?

Yes, that's the most notable thing. The transformation is very obvious. You see it and you realise that there's something else right in front of you, the person being initiated is no longer the same. It's very dramatic.

And how did you deal with all this? You were quite young.

The need and longing I felt was stronger than any fear. You do things for a reason. You don't think about what you're doing, you think about the end goal.

Santería, Umbanda, Voodoo and other religions were brought by slaves from Africa, and these slaves were depressed, they lived in captivity. So, you can guess they didn't use their religion to bless the master's crops. Religion was for self-defence and revenge.

For me it was quite special, because at that moment it gave me the strength to face up to my greatest fear. When I came back from Brazil, I was full of strength and it was just the little shove I needed to go to my mother and say: 'That's enough.' I got home and the next day I told her. And then I left. Without any explanation, I told her I was leaving, and that was it.

And then afterwards, how did religion continue to affect your life?

It didn't. I achieved my goal and I didn't mess with religion again for a long time after that. I took it up again when I went to jail, more as a way of defending myself, of surviving.

Other people have said they saw darkness inside you. What did your mother think of that?

Nothing at all. To her I was a cockroach, a piece of garbage. But she saw nothing dark or negative in me.

One of the theories from the forensic medical team was that if I'd killed my mother, I never would have committed the crimes.

Do you think that's true?

I don't think so.

Did you ever fantasise about killing your mother?

No. Never.

When did you see her last?

When I was twenty years old. For some strange reason I went over to her house, and when I got there, she was with a boyfriend. She had started going out with an evangelical and they were going to get married. In a very formal manner, the guy asked me for my mother's hand in marriage. A crazy idea like that could only have come from her. When I was arrested, my mother was on her honeymoon in Mar del Plata.

Do you ever wonder if she's still alive today?

No. I don't care. If one day I can have a life again, I want to start over, I don't want to have anything to do with any of that. I don't want family, I don't want anything. I just want to be left alone.

KILLING CATS ON FRIDAYS

Very few people know about my history with religion. Well, those who've known me a long time know it all, but apart from that I keep quiet about the whole thing. I'm used to talking with psychiatrists and psychologists who see my beliefs as 'strange religious ideations'. It's just another thing they use to classify me, but still they classify me wrong. That's why I try not to talk about it too much. Many of the employees of the Federal Penitentiary Service are Christians – most of them are evangelicals. So, when it comes to religion, they're very firm about rejecting anything that's not Christianity. Sometimes the evangelicals get to a terrifying level of evangelism. Those people are scary. Truly scary.

Religion here in prison? In the beginning I realised it could be used as a defence, and I fooled around with it for a long time. It started out as a prison joke. In Caseros, I was the crazy kid, the joker of the cell block. One day another inmate came up to me with a tiny coffin, a pretty little thing, painted black. The guy had a hobby, he made little boats out of balsa wood. He came up to me with this coffin and said: 'Look what I made for you, blah blah blah, this, that, the other thing... You wouldn't have a pill, would you?' That's what we call a 'prison rope:' 'You're such a great guy, so smart, you're the best, blah blah blah... You wouldn't have some tomato sauce to cook with, would you?' It's a classic way to swipe things. And, well, I ended up with the coffin in my cell and I said to myself: I'm going to put a doll in it. So I made a little doll and put it in the coffin.

What did you make the doll out of?

Bread crumbs, toilet paper, and blood.

Whose blood?

Mine. I asked the guy to make me three more coffins, and in each of them I put a little doll with the name of my victims. In the cell there was a kind of metal shelf, so I put them all up there and made an altar. And that's how I came up with something that helped protect me. I got lucky stumbling across these things, you know, like when you think school is just a pain in the arse and then all of a sudden the moment comes where you think: 'Fuck, all that shit I learned and couldn't care less about, now it's become useful.' If I, the evil maniac, make a little doll, execute it and hang it from the bars on the cell, then the doll protects me. At the very least, it scares or worries any guy who sees me do it. In Santería, altars and objects are often arranged so that they protect a doorway. Even people with garden gnomes know this. If you look, you'll see garden gnomes are always guarding doors.

It's survival.

Over time, this took off. First it was a couple of inmates who came along with little bits of paper: 'Ricardo, can I leave this with your things, for a little favour I want to ask?' One day we were in the prison yard at Caseros, the big yard. There were some windows that looked out onto the street, and we'd made some holes in the windows so you could pop your head out and speak with visitors, out there in the street. Someone said: '*Che*, a guy down there is asking for you,' so I went down and there was another inmate, one who had left a little bit of paper in my cell and had then been released. He'd come to thank me, as if it was partly due to the paper on my altar that he'd got out. Two hours later, even the guards were leaving little papers on my altar.

There's a lot of superstition in prison. One guy gets released, and straight away another guy wants to sleep in the bed the other guy just left behind. Because that guy got out.

What were the favours the guards asked for?

Mostly they had to do with love or relationships, and lots of favours relating to work: transfers, things like that. At that time the prison guards were savage people, from the interior of the country. There was a joke going around that said that to recruit guards, the Prison Service went out to the mountains in the Chaco, laid ten pairs of boots at the foot of a tree and shook it. Those who fell into the boots became officers, and those who didn't, NCOs.

Perhaps I didn't have that evil streak, or all that prison knowledge, but my cellmates certainly did. 'Oh, the guards don't go into the maniac's cell, they're afraid,' they'd say. 'Let's leave our things in here...' And the guys began to buy into that too, because it served them as well.

In the end there was a consensus that I truly was making these things happen. The inmates, and even the guards too, began to avoid coming into my cell. It was all nonsense, but during shakedowns they went through my altar without touching a thing. The guards had their own mean streak with each other. They'd always send the dumbest one to shakedown my cell: 'Go to the maniac's cell. Touch his things and your hands will fall off.' That's how the legend really took off: 'Maniac, I had to touch your things, it's my job, I did it respectfully, I didn't break anything...'

People say that when I get angry I transform, the look on my face changes, my whole way of being changes. Mystics say I have a force that surrounds me, and they can see it.

Because they're mystics?

Because they're believers. Christians, or believers in some other faith. Believers I came across.

Once, a group of guys got together and began to prepare an escape. They had a gun smuggled in, a small 6.35 calibre pistol with ammunition, as well as a switchblade, and they were waiting for a few more things to arrive. During a routine inspection the bullets were discovered. The guards got nervous, and they began to search through the whole unit looking for the gun. They never found the gun, but they found the switchblade in my cell. There were five of us in the cell, and they put a lot of physical pressure on us during the interrogation, lots of abuse. When it was my turn, I decided on the fly to take responsibility for the switchblade. I said it was mine. They asked me why I had it and I said it was for religious use. 'I use it on Fridays, to kill cats. In my religion we make blood sacrifices.' Besides all that, it wasn't a shiv made in prison, it was a real switchblade brought from the outside. It's very difficult to get a thing like that through security, so they asked me how I got it. 'One of the guards got it for me. He was having trouble with his wife, and I did some couple's therapy for him. In exchange I asked for the knife, because I needed it for the ceremony.' 'What's the guard's name?' 'I'm no snitch, why would I tell you his name?' And so they confiscated the switchblade, but that was the end of the matter.

At that moment, when I made that declaration about the cats and the sacrifices, it was to cover up something bigger, so the guards would leave it there and not delve any further. But there were consequences: the statement was passed up the chain and it ended up in my file. From then on, years would go by and forensic specialists would meet with me and say things like 'How's it going, Melogno, how's the cat hunting going? Any sacrifices lately? Aren't your buddies worried you'll run out of cats one day?' They've never forgotten about that.

Things went along like that until this one time, when I must have been thirty-two or thirty-three years old, and I had been sent to solitary in Unit 20. I had a massive religious experience there, in the sense that I realised that there really was something inside me, in a religious sense. It was something natural, that no one else had taught me...

Like what, for example?

Certain prayers that were deeply ingrained inside me. Or rituals, certain things that I would do at a given time. Little dolls, things that I would make and that worked... On a functional level, the defences I made worked very well in those spaces... So then the big question is WHY do they work...

And then I realised that there were things inside me that led me towards religion. Things like... well, they were already there. My mother never did Voodoo rituals, but I knew how to make Voodoo dolls. I said to myself: shit, how did I do that? Where did I get that from? It wasn't something I'd learned.

I believe that with every reincarnation the soul takes a path that is either purifying or initiatory. I believe that my religious knowledge does not come from this life. I figure my life comes from beforehand, it's a path I've been forging from previous lives, and that the soul preserves any knowledge you acquire. Some things are natural... My understanding, or my madness, makes me believe this.

So, at thirty-two or thirty-three years old, locked away in solitary in Unit 20, I said to myself: I've been fooling and messing around with this stuff for so long. Either I embrace it, accept it and live it seriously, or I let it go. What I mean is it seemed like what I'd been doing up to that point was just deceiving myself through faith and deceiving faith itself. I decided to respect faith, and take it seriously.

Religion isn't about a person who has some kind of existential desire. It's something you already have, something you carry inside you from before. Not because you search for it, but because you've already found it.

KING IN HELL

When did the Devil come into your religious practice?

Santería is difficult to explain. It involves earth spirits and light spirits. The earth spirits are what in Christianity you'd call devils, many of them lived on Earth at one time, and so their evil is of this world, the deceit of this world. There are *candomblés* (songs) from the Quimbanda religion that name Pomba Gira as Lucifer's wife. Pomba Gira has seven personalities, as does Tranca Rua. Pomba Gira is a spirit commonly used for protection by those involved in prostitution, and by transvestites, the same way that criminals have Saint Death or Tranca Rua, the spirit who opens pathways. Tranca Rua is the lord of all roads, he is always in cemeteries, he handles souls. Just like Saint Death, they are pagan saints who intermediate between the living and the spirits.

Well, for me... I never sought intermediaries, I don't have a spirit who connects me to something higher. I would go straight to the source. With my beliefs I didn't want to fall into the sort of mysticism my mother practised at the time.

I don't see the devil as an evil being. I would say that the word 'devil' has been demonised. I see the devil more as a powerful being who helps those who believe in him.

Christianity is a religion driven by fear. I accept Lucifer because he preferred to be a king in hell rather than a slave in heaven. Perhaps though... in my day-to-day, my normal behaviour, my way of thinking... Perhaps I'm more of a Christian than anything else. But that doesn't mean that Lucifer rejects me. Your own faith is one thing, and what others expect from you is quite another. For me religion is one thing, and my behaviour is another. I don't mix them.

In fact, in all these years, I've had lots of dealings with Christians. I had a Christian sponsor, a sponsor from Cáritas who came especially to see me. The people from Cáritas who came to Unit 20 brought *alfajores*, cigarettes, yerba maté, cakes, soda, soap... They knew that everyone in Unit 20 was considered a pariah, and that a lot of us went hungry, and so they tried to improve that. When we were moved here they stopped coming, because the guards steal everything: the food, the nice soda.

Thanks to this sponsor from Cáritas I have a very special trophy. In my religious ceremonies I use a cup for certain things, for certain offerings. For the ceremony, it's important that the cup be made of metal. And for the very last Mass they held in Unit 20, before they closed it, Cáritas brought along Cardinal Bergoglio [now Pope Francis]. Several TV channels came too. My sponsor introduced me to Bergoglio, we spoke for a while, and then he gave me the chalice he had used to celebrate Mass.

He gave it to you for your ceremonies? I mean, did he know what you were going to use it for?

Yeah, he gave it to me so I could use it in my ceremonies. My sponsor had told him what I used to get up to, I don't know... but Bergoglio gave it to me all the same.

So what you're saying is, you have the Pope's chalice and you use it to praise Lucifer and other spirits?

Yeah. It's a cup in the form of a chalice, very simple, unornamented.

Can you describe the look on Bergoglio's face while you were chatting and he started to realise that you prayed to the Devil?

Oh, it wasn't like that at all, he was very chilled... He's from the Franciscan order, he's not a regular priest. It's a different way of thinking. I respect him because he's very respectful in the way he treats others. And there's that time he washed the feet of all the nutcases. He picked out the worst nutcases we had, people who were completely destroyed. It's not like they rounded up the best ones for a little ceremony. The guy went and found the worst of them.

When I pray, more than anything I give thanks. It's like going to a psychologist, you get a problem out in the open to work on it better. Although I live here in this shit, I have an anchor that helps me with the day-to-day, that gives me strength, peace and serenity to go on, and I'm thankful for that.

I'm not one for invocations, because I don't think that prison is the place for that. It's a very dark place. All of the energy in this place is evil; it's a place of madness, pain and suffering. If you invoke something here, you'll only bring suffering, the darkest thing in these surroundings. So I make no invocations. I give thanks and I pray, but I don't make invocations. I've had many cellmates who fool around in here: 'Hey, let's play the game with the cup...' And things like that. No. Not even as a joke in here.

Outside, in a temple, I'd celebrate the proper days, I'd make the proper offerings of drinks, with the correct mix. In here, because I don't have the right things nor the opportunity to go to the right place to do it, I offer what I have and what I can. And perhaps my offerings are more impassioned and truer than those I could make on the outside. If I spend a week without smoking so that I can offer cigarettes, or I give up eating something that is very important to me, like a chocolate that is very difficult to get hold of, it's an offering of my sacrifice. I'm giving something that is very difficult to obtain, because in here whatever I offer has great value. I offer up something that it hurts to be without. What's more, it's something I see the whole time, because it's sitting there on the altar all day, right in front of me.

What happens to the offerings? Do they stay there on the altar?

The altar gets cleaned once a month. When I was in Unit 20 I could burn the offerings, that was possible. Here, unfortunately, there's nowhere to burn anything, so I throw them away. Anyway, I use lots of packaged things, because the altar is in my cell, next to my bed, and it'd be crawling with bugs... In the outside world, offerings are left in town squares, on the ground, beneath trees.

Speaking of your altar... What about using documents to protect against the souls of your victims? Do you still do that?

No, I don't do that anymore. I can't remember the photos of the people I killed. I don't recall ever having seen their faces. Their spirits never came to bother me or demand anything from me.

At this stage, there's only one thing I'm going to try to take care of. Not in terms of my thoughts, but... well, the thing is, to try... not to hurt anyone with my memories.

What do you mean by that?

[*Melogno reflects for a few seconds*]

The victims had families. You understand what I'm saying, right? I don't want to offend those people.

Did you ever hear anything from any of the families?

No. But just in case, I want to be very clear. Beyond all the excuses, all the... not excuses, the mitigating factors that there might be in my case... I did commit those murders.

Are you making a sort of moral evaluation about it all?

There's no evaluation, these are facts.

In terms of reincarnation, have you ever thought you might come across those taxi drivers? Have you ever fantasised about that?

We will all meet again at some point. So the answer is yes. It's not something I fantasise about, it's something that is definitely going to happen. But I also believe that there will be no judgement on the other side, because those men are already living other lives. And that goes for me too – after I die, I'll be someone else. In every reincarnation you come across the same people... that's why when you have a strange affinity with someone, often it's because... The thing is, the person who is your lover today, in the next reincarnation, they could be your brother. Or your butcher.

STATISTICALLY UNUSUAL

[*M.R. is a psychiatrist. She treated Ricardo for seven years in Unit 20 of the Borda Hospital.*]

Weird how?

He doesn't seem like a serial killer.

Were you expecting someone in a leather mask, carrying a chainsaw?

Maybe not that exactly, but... he seems more like a pencil pusher than a serial killer.

Haha, it's not a bad image, the poor guy...

Is he, in fact, a serial killer?

Considering there were four murders, that the victims and methodology follow a specific pattern, and that there is a certain spacing between incidents... You could say the answer is yes. But, going by what Ricardo has said, one important element that defines a serial killer is missing, and that's the period where the homicidal impulse between crimes recedes. He speaks of an inertia, a slightly more continuous impulse.

Apart from that, with serial killings, generally there are elements that evolve from murder to murder. 'Series' means a succession of terms that vary from a fixed base. There's a fixed element, but this element evolves in some aspects. In this case, rather than a series, it's more like the same crime repeated four times, almost identically.

For me, this almost falls outside the existing classifications for multiple homicides. Of course, these definitions are poor as well, because the studies are made from a very small sample space. Very strange people, very unusual in statistical terms. In a normal distribution of the total population, murderers we might deem 'irrational', those who don't kill for pedestrian reasons like jealousy or money, are right at the end of the curve. It's a tiny population in numerical terms. And Ricardo... Well, I'd say if you put together a Gaussian distribution that only featured irrational murderers, Ricardo would be on the extreme of that curve too. He's a very unusual person, even when considered within a population of unusual people.

What makes him so unusual?

First, there's the series of contradictory diagnoses across the years. They've been contradictory and they've never quite described him fully. Second, there's the lack of motive for his actions, and the impossibility of inferring them. His lack of deterioration is also noteworthy. Nearly every diagnosis he's been given implies functional deterioration over time, which he doesn't show. Every diagnosis except psychopathy.

Is he a psychopath?

Personally, having treated him for several years, I don't think so. In terms of concrete behaviour, he's not a predator, he's not a parasite. He has a certain degree of empathy – I've seen him become upset hearing about the circumstances of others, I've seen him help out. If a psychopath talks to you, it's to use you, or because they want to enjoy something they're about to do to you. That's not the case with Ricardo. He's not manipulative, he's not a liar. He tells you what's going on, and often he'll tell you things that don't work in his favour. My interpretation of this is that he's on the autism spectrum. He responds in concrete terms. You ask him something and he answers. He understands things literally, and he kind of responds literally to whatever you ask him. In fact, he makes an effort to find an answer.

So why is there this diagnosis of psychopathy?

When they found no delirious responses, when they failed to see him in a psychotic state (he doesn't rant or rave, or speak incoherently) some medical professionals took this to mean he was a psychopath. He's intelligent, if that's something that can be associated with psychopaths. And that's where the fact that he's respectful and on good terms with prison staff comes in. Sometimes psychiatrists see this as a sign of psychopathic adaptation, but that's a very weak argument.

The last time he was diagnosed with psychopathy in the courts in the Province of Buenos Aires was relatively recently, just when the courts in the City of Buenos Aires lifted their safety restrictions on him and he could begin to ask for supervised excursions. Then the Province declared he had a contracted illness. For them Ricardo had been normal all this time, conscious and responsible for his actions.

An illness contracted from what?

From his time in prison. An illness he theoretically contracted in prison, and which prevents him from leaving. In other words, according to them, he recently acquired, as an adult, an illness (psychopathy), which in fact is not an illness, it's a stable condition that doesn't change. They diagnosed him with it out of fear, because they were going to have to let him out, and they were too afraid to sign off on his release.

There is one very notable thing, no small matter, which is his lack of injuries in prison. It's very strange, and I must stress VERY strange, for an individual to have suffered no wounds from fighting with other inmates in over thirty-five years of jail time.

What is the likelihood that he would have continued killing if he hadn't been arrested?

That's controversial... There are people who say he'd already stopped, that it had been over two weeks since his last murder when they locked him up. I have my reservations about that. If someone has a psychotic break, it's difficult for them to come back without medication, without confinement. There's a common saying in psychiatry: walls (of the hospital, or the prison) hold things in. They hold in everything a patient's head can't. A psychiatrist and a psychologist are also a kind of confinement, a dike for the mental structures that are falling down, that become blurred and confuse reality with fantasy.

Is he still dangerous?

He's stable. He's not a violent person and he hasn't shown any predatory behaviour in over thirty years. I don't think he'd do what he did again, given the same circumstances. Of course, he is still capable of killing, but by now the probability that he would kill would be about the same as for you or me. Have you ever seriously fantasised about killing someone?

Of course.

Good. Me too. And I'll tell you something else: when I say I fantasise about killing, I'm talking about killing a specific, actual person. A person with a first and last name. Someone I know very well. Twice a month I go to a shooting range. I'm no crack shot, but I make do, I can group my shots together tightly. Every time I go, I use up two boxes of bullets. And each time I pull the trigger, I'm thinking of that person. Now, I'm not actually planning to physically kill them when I do this. But each time I shoot at a target, in my mind I'm shooting that person right in the head. Four boxes of .22 calibre bullets every month. If we look at the facts, Ricardo committed four murders, and I've committed none. But in the current situation, it's possible I'm more dangerous than he is. And yet here we are, chatting away.

ELECTRICITY AND MAGNETISM

September 1982. The dead of night, at a dark crossroads in Lomas del Mirador. On one of the four corners, there's a taxi parked a few centimetres away from the sidewalk. Inside the car, for a brief moment, the passage of time has somehow come to a halt.

The taxi driver is dead. There's a bullet in his head and his body is slumped in the front seat, leaning towards the passenger side. At the edge of the scene, in the back seat, a young man around twenty years old holds a .22 calibre pistol that's still smoking. He's paralysed with terror: he has just discovered that he is being *observed*. From the rear-view mirror, strange eyes stare at him intensely.

While this instant remains frozen in time, a correspondence is produced between these two gazes. On the watery film covering the eyes watching him from the mirror, he is reflected dark and convex in the interior of the taxi. In miniature, above the centre of the pupils, you can see the face of the young passenger who stares on, hypnotised, at the rear-view mirror, like a deer caught in headlights that shatter the darkness of the night. If you could zoom into the pupils on his face, once more you would see the reflection of those eyes watching him from the rear-view mirror. Inside the eyes, the young man's face again, and so on: one image inside another image, a series of reflections opposing one another. Reality itself shrivelling away.

THURSDAY
PATRÍCIA PORTELA
tr. RAHUL BERY

'Not my name. I live on the streets of an era in which saying one's name is a cause for suspicion... The name I bear today may not recognise me tomorrow. So I do not bind my face to a particular name.'
João Gilberto Noll

This is how it begins. When it seems as if it's all over.

Staring at the ground without blinking, I notice a piece of damp earth that seems like it's in the wrong place. I pick it up with both hands and without really knowing why, I put the fistful of damp earth that's in the wrong place in my pocket, and decide to walk until I know where I'm trying to get to.

Maybe to a place where this bit of earth fits.

I pass by a neighbour's house, knock on the door, and while I'm waiting for them to answer, I notice the outline of a perfect rectangle on the ground where a doormat has been removed. Without really knowing why, other than the strong smell that seems to be coming from it, I push the outline of the mat further down into the tightly packed earth and exchange the damp earth in my pockets for a dry clump. I fill both pockets again and depart, as if I've just left a message.

I go up a hill. I dig a hole to leave the dry earth in and take a bit of quartz stone which, I don't know if you know, is the most common stone on our planet and can be used to make many things: soap, toothpaste, sandpaper, optic fibres, watches, radios, ashtrays, even cheap jewellery.

I don't want to do anything with this stone, I just want to carry it. I pick up the stone which also smells of damp earth and don't look back.

For reasons not worth mentioning, I move on.

Some would say: I depart.

But I say: I split.

I arrive at the border between my city and the next.

A river separates the two. I feel my quartz stone works perfectly as a border marker. I put it down by the river's edge and fill my pockets with shells from the bank.

I continue.

In this city I have no neighbours whose doors I can knock on.

I come to a halt at a bus stop by an abandoned quarry. I crush the shells into a fine powder which I try to insert into the cracks in the stones, exchanging them for a lovely piece of marble. It's too heavy to carry on foot, so it's lucky I'm near a bus stop. I get on the first bus that looks as if it's going somewhere far away. I doze during the journey and wake to find someone asking to see my passport. I have no real reason to be scared, but I am, very much so, and without really knowing how, nor why, I hide. Behind the marble. At the first opportunity, I flee. I walk the whole night, dragging my portion of earth, which is made of stone, and by the time I get to a place that's far away from the place I've escaped from, it's getting dark again. It occurs to me that I might now be in another country, otherwise they wouldn't have asked for my passport. Some countries are so small, you can lose them just like that, even when they're difficult to enter or leave. The distance is never the issue.

There's not a living soul to be seen in this far-off place, which may well be another country. Without really knowing what brings me there, I knock on the first door I find, probably a government office. As there's no one around, without thinking twice I set down the marble on the counter and take a piece of slate from a blackboard lying there on the floor, propped up against a wall. I keep going until I arrive in another city, maybe even a third country. There's not a single flowerbed. Everything is set upon structures made of steel and concrete. I find a drill and a yellow high-vis suit, neither of which seems to belong to anyone. I choose a motorway under construction so that I can go about as I please for a few days, in my discreet, fluorescent uniform. I join a team of workers who are all apparently as foreign as I am and help them with the more arduous tasks. No one asks any questions. By the third day I'm sharing my lunch with the team and at three in the afternoon I choose my place, right by the entrance of a service station. With the drill, I cut out a piece of tarmac. It takes me a few hours, but the result far exceeds my expectations. In the tarmac's place I drop the piece of slate from the office. I water it, just as I'd water any other piece of earth, and I inaugurate this new territory by putting up a red and white ribbon around it to keep out trespassers. I keep a bit of tarmac to take with me. I depart immediately in the hope of quickly finding a new resting place, for it's summer and this piece of road is hot.

Before I've even walked half a dozen kilometres, I notice a wall.

That divides a city.

That divides a country.

That divides an entire world in two.

I crush the piece of tarmac against the cement and use it to fill the cracks in an extremely high wall that is due to be demolished, and I take a piece of wall the same size as the tarmac, all broken up into tiny pieces, like little souvenirs. I continue on to the next country and when I get there I find another wall which, because it's bigger, because it's older, and because it defends a king from enemy attacks while stemming the exodus of the poorest people, is called a rampart, and as I'm getting ready to exchange several bits of graffiti-covered wall for an ancient pebble, I remember that this rampart may be protected, because it is used in the telling of an official story, and so cannot be demolished. Stripped of my belongings and documents, it doesn't seem wise for me to challenge patrimony; so I scrape off all the lichen and seal the holes in a ruined tower with my brick and cement.

With all the moss I can carry, I keep heading north, to a tundra.

To one side, trees. To the other, polar ice. I feel like the moss goes well with the ice. With a pick, I split open an iceberg, which immediately comes unstuck, sliding off towards the south, with me on top of it, at a speed I find simply astonishing for an iceberg, considering their tendency to move extremely slowly.

The journey is long and the iceberg does not withstand the increase in temperature, so it melts, raising the sea level with it. In a flooded land, still drifting, I rest. I wake up and realise that the earth around me has dried up, and is now made of salt. Partially buried, my hands touch a piece of mosaic under the salt. I can feel it. An empire beneath the salt: chambers, atria, springs, roads, houses, tables, candelabra, emperors, vendors, tax collectors, prostitutes, all intact, frozen in time, as if in brine. And beneath the empire, a sheet of lava.

For a few short moments I convince myself that I've sailed into the earth's crust, all the way through to the opposing hemisphere, getting to the other side without going all the way round. This beautiful image notwithstanding, knowing where I am doesn't seem that important.

I set foot upon the empire, and exchange the salt for basalt.

At this exact moment, the pillaging begins.

Men appear, seemingly from nowhere, and lay waste to what remains of the empire, in search of relics, precious jewels, antiques, food, shelter. A market springs up on this saline soil, above an empire, above a cloak of lava. Without leaving the place, I exchange the basalt for limestone, which I exchange for granite, which I exchange for lead, which I exchange for iron, which I exchange for zinc, which I exchange for bronze, which I exchange for pewter, which I exchange for silver, which I exchange for jade, which I exchange for nickel, which I exchange for phosphorus, which I exchange for uranium, which, I don't know if you know, is a radioactive element, white and combustible, number 92 on the periodic table, and which we once used as a yellowish dye before we found out it could cause nuclear explosions.

I grab the uranium and take it to an atoll.

I sit down, facing the sea. To plant uranium on a beach is no easy task, in fact I think it's illegal unless a government has told you to do it. I choose a location set back from the shore, and dig metres and metres down, days and days of arduous labour beneath a blazing sun, without eating or sleeping, until I reach the first layer of rock. I bury my potential nuclear explosion. I take the sand I've dug out with me. I board an inflatable boat and enter the terrible, unrelenting sea, and as I travel it occurs to me that the sea is also a country. I exchange the sand crystals for crystalline water. I do my sums and fill the boat with litres and litres of salty waves. I'm so focused on what I'm doing that I forget boats can't hold that much water, especially when there are people in them.

And so I sink.

You'd say: I'm shipwrecked.

I hit the bottom. That's what happens.

Strangely, I can still breathe at the bottom. Carried along by the kind of current that is said to carry turtles on their annual migrations to Australia, I enter a cave. I lose consciousness. Of myself and of the purpose of my journey. I come to on a beach, clinging to a piece of abyssolith, a rock so old and so fossilised that it can tell our story from the earth's very beginnings, and yet we don't even notice it, perhaps because we don't want to know.

I'm not in Australia, I think. But I am on an island which trembles when I drop the abyssolith. I open my eyes and I'm alone again, standing before a lifeless body. The thought occurs to me that a body is also a country, that it too smells of wet earth.

I grab the body, kiss it like I'm in love with it, and bury it in a church said to be the birthplace of every prophet of every doctrine, though officially it belongs to just one of them.

I bury the body under the right side of the nave and get ready to take a slab of stone with no name on it. When I get up there's a man behind me, and he grabs me by the neck and asks who I am. I say my name, but that's not what he wants, he wants the name of the dead person, which I don't know, and when he squeezes my throat and suggests a name, I repeat that I don't know, that I found the body in another country, in another city, no, an island, in a hole that had abyssolith in it, and he keeps squeezing my throat, and as I struggle to breathe it occurs to me that death can also be a country, an interminable country with no borders, no languages, a country I do not want to live in just yet. I grab my death by the horns and throw it at the man who is strangling me. It's a simple reflex, one that neither demands courage, nor brings satisfaction. Now, regardless of my own personal feelings, it seems wise to change country, above all because our stories are always different when told by other people, and I don't want to risk anyone comparing my story with someone else's.

I run all night long, hoping I'm running in the right direction, and I reach yet another border which, for reasons again unknown to me (even if they weren't, they'd make no sense to anyone who is not running for their life, like me), I show the passport of the man I threw my death at, pay for my visa with his money, go from being a woman to being a man, and cross the border, bearing the load of the stone with no name on my back.

Identity is a kind of country too. A temporary one, but a country nevertheless. It's not a body, it's not a piece of land, it's not an ocean, it may not be our own identity, but nevertheless it's still a country of sorts.

Across the border, someone is standing before me, and they say: 'I've been waiting for you.' I don't understand her language but I understand what she's trying to tell me. She calls me by what I presume is the name of the man with whom I exchanged my death, gives me her arm, we feel a tiny electric shock when our shoulders, encased in nylon, meet, and then she takes me to her house. I exchange my woman's body and the body of the man I killed for a living body. I begin to doubt my own intentions behind the initial exchange of earth. I get some clean clothes and take a hot bath. The wedding takes place the following day. I try to explain myself, but only false justifications escape from my mouth, and her religion doesn't permit questions. I begin reading out loud in order to clarify my misunderstandings, and when the morning comes I exchange the slab for brick, and the brick for a roof tile, and I build a house, a family, a new language, a dog, a garden, a job in the family business. We won't have children.

But I start again. So I think.

You're mistaken, I hear you say.

In reality, I'm never the same again.

Everything loses its urgency and becomes habit.

I go along with it, but on the inside I'm still running as fast as I can.

I wake before dawn, drenched in the sweat of my nocturnal marathons.

In the mornings I slow down almost to the point of paralysis. And I'm beginning to repeat myself. I am my own earth, and every day I exchange myself. Then one day it happens again: I wake up even earlier than usual and notice that the earth smells not like earth, but like that one piece of wet earth. My eyes are soaking wet. I stop myself from getting up until I find a solution. I just lie there, listening, feeling. I hear an explosion. I go out on to the streets in my pyjamas, carrying a torch, to find the engine-room door wide open, with all the wires cut. The smell is coming from in there, but not just from in there. I look at the cables again, remember that cables also contain earth, and think: that's it! I strip the wires and the cables and repeat the explosion that had woken me up. Oil pours from the earth where we've built our home, our family, our language, our garden, my job, the business which has no heirs to run it in the future. Petrol is not easy to transport but it can easily be exchanged for any other kind of earth, that much is obvious. And suddenly I'm not alone, though everyone is a stranger. They speak to me in a language I understand but which belongs neither to them nor to me, asking me what I'm doing there. I don't know how to respond. I realise I'm in a fix, and only then do I think to ask myself: Can it be that they also know the cables are earth? Sometimes we make decisions that come from nowhere and which we cannot stop, and I feel an uncontrollable urge to prove my existence by gently beating the earth with my hands as I answer the only question they don't ask me and I tell them I urgently need to measure our current, our resistance, our voltage, to understand where it is we're all going and when. I raise my eyes, and she responds, my wife who's not there, and I see her being escorted by these unknown men, and in an attempt to change the topic of conversation or maybe to pursue it further, she tells me that my problem is simply one of alterity. I realise that what follows is one more attempt at restitution, not of the earth or the current but of the truth, and it's then I hear her say, 'Being with me turns you into someone else, doesn't it?', and I don't know what to say because I know what awaits me and she continues, 'Being with me lifts you up from yourself, like a hoisting cable, just as other cables keep us connected to the ground'. 'That's it, that's exactly it,' I say. Things have a strange way of being understood even in the most unexpected circumstances. Before I realise it I find myself in a car boot with my hands bound and a bandage covering my eyes. I'm struggling to think and so I let things be for a moment, finding out if what's happening to me is actually happening. When I come round, it smells of earth again – a very strong odour this time, of burnt earth.

I decide I'm in a film, that this isn't really happening to me, and I think of Harrison Ford, who's so good at freeing himself when his hands are bound with rope, always dragging himself along to a sharp object and thus dealing with the situation. So, like Harrison Ford, I drag myself along on the ground. And I do in fact manage to free myself, not because I find a sharp object but because the earth around me is burning and the fire burns my hands and burns through the ropes. Instinctively I put my hands to the ground to put out the flames (funny how the earth lights fires but also extinguishes them, it's like it can't make its mind up), and then I bring them to my eyes to rip off the bandage; I fill the pockets of my shirt, trousers and coat with ashes. I don't know if I want to go back to the house I own, the house I owned, or to the house I'd like to have found.

I think we all suffer from mild cases of aporia, the tremendous difficulty in choosing between two contrary opinions on the same principle; and when there is no space to think, one simply runs.

So I run.

And I'm still running.

Arriving.

Going towards that familiar border.

I realise that the identity I now possess (which was once someone else's) does not allow me to enter into that country which may well once have been mine. I want to re-enter, I really do, for the first time it makes so much sense, it makes all the difference, for reasons obvious only to me (which should more than suffice). I don't want to go anywhere else, I want to go there, that is, here, and when I'm refused entry I head to the customs office, and tell them I've come from a country at war and am seeking political asylum from my former country. I fill out a form, sign it, get a passport photo taken and, exchanging the ashes of the fire I put out for the dust on the bench in the customs office I become a citizen of a country I've never been to as a woman, in order to seek political asylum from my own country, where they speak my own language.

I go out on to the streets, overcome with the happiness of someone who does not know what they're doing but is convinced they're doing the right thing, and I take a look around. Lorries are arriving and departing, taking many pieces of earth from many countries to many others. I stand there while the earth moves on its own, without me. Without a soul.

And I watch cement being exchanged for clay being exchanged for painted tiles being exchanged for crystal being exchanged for porcelain being exchanged for tea being exchanged for opium being exchanged for cotton being exchanged for coffee being exchanged for spices being exchanged for amber being exchanged for resin being exchanged for honey being exchanged for sugar cane being exchanged for palm oil being exchanged for butter being exchanged for seeds being exchanged for roots being exchanged for coal being exchanged for gas being exchanged for sulphur which, I don't know if you knew, perfumes the depths of hell, is essential for living organisms, and is used to make fertilisers, insecticides, laxatives, gunpowder and matchstick heads.

One day so much of the world will have been exchanged that we'll feel at home anywhere. As I think about this, I suddenly notice that I'm in a lorry, I must have got in without thinking, and the lorry sets off with me inside, and I'm picked up at a roadside check with a declaration in my pocket confirming I come from a country that is at war and am therefore illegal in this country which, despite being my own land, has still not offered me asylum. I'm deported to an unknown country, one I've never been to, but which my papers insist is my own country; the earth there smells completely different from all the earth I've collected up to this point.

It no longer makes any sense to stop.

I sell my declaration of citizenship of a country at war for a tent, in the middle of a savannah. I hammer in the first peg and find a diamond. I sell the first one, sell the second one, sell the third and fourth, and exchange the ones that follow for a bigger mine, which I exchange for an even more valuable one, which I exchange for weapons with which to defend my business (and to buy every passport going at gunpoint), which I exchange for even more money, which I exchange for a private plane, so that I can exchange many lands for many others, which I accidentally exchange for 1,000 millibars of atmospheric pressure, which is exchanged for many many decibels when I crash into the first plateau that resembles mine, at least from afar. I think to myself: I've arrived!

I try to enter my house but the door is locked. It has other walls, other windows. I look for my keys. I forget that I exchanged them for two spades for two coffees for three nights' sleep for an overall for two sheets for a fridge for three bowls of soup, basically, to survive. I have no keys. I knock on the door. Inside someone shouts that they're closed for lunch. From outside I explain that I used to live there. Inside they reply that no one has lived here for a long time. I ignore what they tell me and inside they keep saying, 'Yes, this is the right place, but it's not yours, it's a government office now'. 'Wait there,' I say, 'Yes, it's mine, but it wasn't right there, it was more over that way'. 'It may well have been,' the person inside says, 'but the fact is that now it's a government office'. 'This makes no sense,' I think, and as if the person inside has heard me, they reply, 'It may not make sense, but we own the land, we own the house, we have the key, it's ours now, and if you wouldn't mind, please stop bothering us, don't you see we're on our lunch break?'

I'm speechless, something almost as serious as being landless. I take the opportunity to go over to what may have been my first flowerbed in front of what may not be my house.

And that's when my courage fails.

I sit down, to avoid falling over. I remember that it all began when I decided to run against the wind. And once again the wind decided to run against me. And it changed the way the earth smells. I find a ring. It's not mine. But it reminds me of one I lost there. Perhaps time is also earth, also a country, one bigger than all the others, soaring above all of them, as it accumulates every state on earth before occasionally letting one fall, like residual pieces of places in places of places, in places where these places never were until now. How can the earth be made of a single word, when so many others fit inside it?

RAHUL BERY is a translator from Spanish and Portuguese into English, based in Cardiff. His translations have appeared in *Granta*, *The White Review*, *Words Without Borders* and *Latin American Literature Today*, among others. He is currently Translator in Residence at the British Library.

LEO BOIX is a bilingual poet, translator and journalist born in Argentina who lives and works in the UK. Boix has published two poetry collections in Spanish and has been included in many anthologies, such as *Ten: Poets of the New Generation* (Bloodaxe), *Why Poetry?* (Verve Poetry Press), and the forthcoming *Islands Are But Mountains: Contemporary Poetry from Great Britain* (Platypus Press) and *British LatinX Writers* (Flipped Eye). His poems in English have appeared in *POETRY*, *PN Review*, *The Poetry Review*, *Modern Poetry in Translation*, *The Manchester Review*, *PRISM International*, *The Laurel Review* and elsewhere. Boix is a fellow of The Complete Works Program and co-director of Invisible Presence, an Arts Council funded national scheme to nurture young Latino-British poets.

JOHN BOUGHTON is a social historian whose book *Municipal Dreams: the Rise and Fall of Council Housing* was published by Verso in April 2018 and recommended as an *Observer* Book of the Year. His popular blog, also called *Municipal Dreams*, which charts the history of council estates up and down the country, has had over 1.1 million views. He has published in the *Historian* and *Labor History* and gives talks on housing to a range of audiences. He is involved in a number of housing campaigns and lives in London.

DANIEL COHEN is a regular contributor to the *Guardian* and *Financial Times*. He lives in London.

KAYE DONACHIE (b. 1970, Glasgow) is an artist living and working in London, UK. Her recent solo exhibitions include *Like this. Before. Like waves*, Morena di Luna, Hove, UK; *Silent As Glass*, Maureen Paley, London, 2018; *Under the clouds of her eyelids*, Le Plateau Frac ile-de-France, Paris, France, 2017 and *Dearest...*, The Fireplace Project, East Hampton, USA, 2015. Selected group exhibitions include *Orlando at the present time*, The Wolfson Gallery, Charleston, East Sussex, UK, 2018, and *The Critic as Artist*, curated by Michael Bracewell

and Andrew Hunt, Reading International, Reading, UK, 2017.

CARLOS FONSECA is a writer and academic. He is the author of two novels. His first novel, *Coronel Lágrimas*, translated by Megan McDowell, was published in English by Restless Books. His second novel, *Museo animal*, is forthcoming in English from FSG. His book of essays *La lucidez del miope* won the National Prize of Literature of Costa Rica. He teaches at Cambridge and lives in London.

CHARLOTTE GEATER lives in London and works for The Emma Press. She recently completed a PhD at the University of Kent. Her poetry has previously been published in *Clinic*, *Strange Horizons* and *The Best British Poetry 2013*. She won the 2018 White Review Poet's Prize for the poems published here.

EDWARD HERRING received his MFA from Washington University in St Louis, where he was Junior Writer in Residence (Fiction) 2015-16. An earlier version of *RLT* was exhibited last year in 'Low Entertainment' at Arch 5.

JANET HONG is a writer and translator based in Vancouver, Canada. She received the 2018 TA First Translation Prize for her translation of Han Yujoo's *The Impossible Fairy Tale*, which was also a finalist for both the 2018 PEN Translation Prize and the 2018 National Translation Award. She has translated Ha Seong-nan's *Flowers of Mold*, Ancco's *Bad Friends*, and Keum Suk Gendry-Kim's *Grass*.

SERAPHIMA KENNEDY is a poet, memoirist and journalist born in west London. Her poems have been published in *The Rialto*, *Magma* and *And Other Poems* and she has performed at the Ledbury Poetry Festival and Poetry in Aldeburgh. In 2017, she was selected for the Jerwood Arvon mentoring programme and was also shortlisted for The White Review Poet's Prize. She is a journalist and writes comment for the *Guardian*. She is a member of the collective Malika's Poetry Kitchen.

LORNA MACINTYRE (b. 1977, Glasgow) is an artist with a varied practice which draws upon literature, poetry, archaeology and mythology. She creates both photographic and sculptural works, which see materials pushed to develop in unexpected ways, allowing chance and process to take pivotal roles. Macintyre has exhibited widely, including solo exhibitions at Mount Stuart, Isle of Bute; Wiels, Brussels; Kunsthaus Baselland; ICA, London and most recently Dundee Contemporary Arts, in late 2018.

SO MAYER is the author of three feminist film books, and several poetry collections, most recently ‹jacked a kaddish› (Litmus, 2018) and (O) (Arc, 2015), and a collaborative essay, with Preti Taneja, *Tender Questions* (Peninsula Press, 2018). They are a bookseller at Burley Fisher Books, a curator with queer feminist collective Club des Femmes, and a co-founder of activist group Raising Films. Current projects include the tiny-letter *Disturbing Words*, and a book-length sequence of Medusa poems following on from *kaolin or, How Does a Girl Like You Get to Be a Girl Like You* (Lark, Oakland CA, 2015).

BRIDGET MINAMORE is a British-Ghanaian writer from south-east London. She is a poet, critic, essayist, and journalist, writing for the *Guardian* about pop culture, theatre, race and class. *Titanic* (Out-Spoken Press), her debut pamphlet of poems on modern love and loss, was published in May 2016.

CHRISTINE OKOTH is a Research Fellow at the University of Warwick and is writing a book about ecology, extraction, and contemporary literature.

PATRÍCIA PORTELA is a writer and performance maker, living between Belgium and Portugal. She studied set and costume design in Lisbon, scenography in Utrecht, The Netherlands, film in Ebeltoft, Denmark and Helsinki, Finland, and Philosophy in Leuven, Belgium. She won the Revelation Prize in 1994 for her creative work in performance and cinema, the Prize Teatro na Década for *T5* in 1999, the Gulbenkian Foundation Prize Madalena de Azeredo Perdigão for the performance *Flatland I* in 2004 and was one of the five finalists of the Sonae Media Art Prize 2015 with her installation *Parasomnia*, amongst other prizes. She is the author of novels including *Banquet* (finalist for the APEL Novel Prize 2012), and has been a writer for the prestigious *Jornal de Letras* since 2017. The story in this issue is taken from her 2017 collection *Dias Úteis* (Working Days), which contains one story for each day of the week.

SAMUEL RUTTER is a writer and translator from Melbourne, Australia. He has translated several works of fiction from authors including Selva Almada, Hernán Ronsino, and Sònia Hernández. His translation of Carlos Busqued's *Magnetised* is forthcoming with Catapult in 2020.

KANG YOUNG-SOOK is an important South Korean feminist writer. Since her debut in 1998, she has published close to a dozen novels and short story collections, including *Rina*, *At Night He Lifts Weights*, *Black in Red*, and *Writing Club*, among many others. She has also received numerous prestigious awards, such as the Hanguk Ilbo Literature Prize, the Kim Yujeong Literary Award, and the Lee Hyo-seok Literature Award. She participated in the International Writing Program's fall residency at the University of Iowa in 2009, and was a visiting writer-in-residence at UC Berkeley in 2014. She currently teaches creative writing at Ewha Womans University and Korea National University of Arts.

PLATES

Insurrecto by Gina Apostol
is published by Fitzcarraldo Editions
on 17 July 2019.

'Gina Apostol – a smart writer, a sharp
critic, a keen intellectual – takes on the
vexed relationship between the Philippines
and the United States, pivoting on that
relationship's bloody origins. *Insurrecto*
is meta-fictional, meta-cinematic, even
meta-meta, plunging us into the vortex of
memory, history, and war where we can feel
what it means to be forgotten, and what it
takes to be remembered.'

— Viet Thanh Nguyen, author
of *The Sympathizer*

Fitzcarraldo Editions

GOLDSMITHS CENTRE FOR CONTEMPORARY ART

ST JAMES'
LONDON SE14 6AD
GOLDSMITHSCCA.ART

ISSY WOOD
28 JUN - 11 AUG 2019

JEF CORNELIS
28 JUN - 11 AUG 2019

COREY HAYMAN
17 JUL - 11 AUG 2019

TONY COKES
28 SEP 2019
- 12 JAN 2020

FREE ENTRY TO ALL
EXHIBITIONS

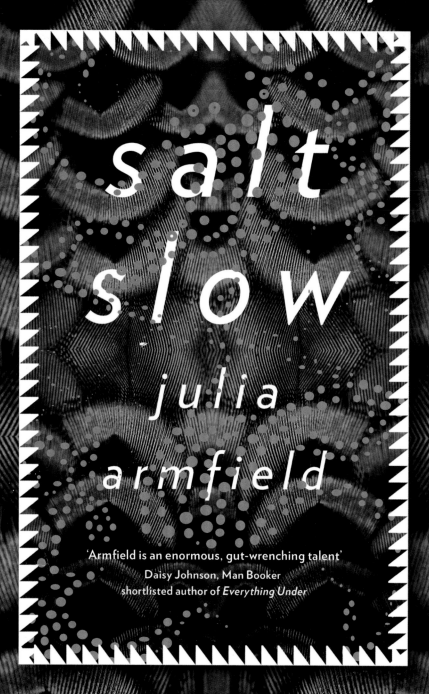

salt slow

julia armfield